RANCHER'S CHRISTMAS COWGIRL

TRINITY FALLS SWEET ROMANCE - BOOK 9

CLARA PINES

PINE NUT PRESS

Copyright © 2023 by Pine Nut Press

All rights reserved. This book or any portion thereof may not be reproduced or used in any manner whatsoever without the express written permission of the publisher except for the use of brief quotations in a book review.

Pine Nut Press

PO Box 506

Swarthmore, PA 19081

pinenutpress@gmail.com

Cover designed by The Book Brander

1

EMMA

Emma Williams stood on the edge of the field in two inches of mud, watching her favorite horse eye her curiously while he nibbled at the last of the green grass just past the fence line.

Clifford was elderly now—the sway of his back and his jutting hip bones gave that away immediately. But he had been the storybook stallion of Emma's childhood—big and red and gentle, though he hadn't been young even then.

Early this morning, a rotted section of the wooden fencing had given way, allowing him and the other horses on the Williams Homestead a rare taste of complete freedom. And although Clifford was normally a laidback gentleman, even he couldn't resist sampling the forest grass just outside the pasture.

Emma had spent most of the morning wrangling the rest of them back to the stables. Her legs ached, and she had stubbed her toe hard on a rock while launching herself at Duke, the young bay. She wanted nothing more than to sink into a chair with a steaming cup of hot coffee.

But now that it was Clifford's turn to be brought in, she

found herself wanting to give him a minute instead of just rushing to get the job done.

I won't be any trouble at all, he seemed to be telling her. *It's just that I've wanted a little taste of this grass for years.*

"Always greener on the other side, huh, Cliff?" she asked him out loud.

He flicked his ears but kept eating.

She smiled at him, and then glanced up at the sky.

The sun was too high. The morning had slipped away just like the horses, and Emma still had chores to do, plus she had to fit in a trip to the feed shop.

"Okay, big boy," she told him after a moment. "We have to go in now."

Clifford pretended to ignore her, but his ears were pricked up and he didn't try to run. When she offered him a cube of sugar he allowed himself to be coaxed back without a fight.

She gave him a good scratch behind the ears, and he nudged his muzzle into her belly fondly, snuffling a little, before they headed in.

Holding Clifford's harness and walking back to the barn with the familiar sounds and smells of the farm all around them, Emma felt almost untethered from time itself. She had walked the path between the pasture and the stables with him so many times, for so many years, that she only had to close her eyes to be eight years old again.

There was something comforting about things remaining constant, and something worrisome about it, too.

Would she be as sway-backed and elderly as Clifford the next time she blinked? Would her life still feel the same after all that time? And would that be so bad?

Emma had always loved the farm and her parents. She

loved working with two of her big brothers every day. It wasn't like there was anything wrong with putting in an honest day's labor. And she lived on a beautiful historic homestead, even if the old houses were a bit run-down these days.

It was a fairytale life and exactly the one she wanted. The only trouble was that she had never known anything else.

While her friends went off to college, Emma had been thrilled to be able to spend all her time on the farm after high school. Her parents had encouraged her to enroll at the community college right in Trinity Falls, but she had put it off, and now a couple of years had passed. It would be weird to be a freshman in her twenties.

And besides, what would she study? She already had her dream job, and she learned more from her daily work and the guys down at the feed shop than she ever could at school.

Honestly, she had no idea why there was a tickle of restlessness in her heart lately. Things were pretty great just the way they were. She'd be lucky to still be doing this when she was a little old lady.

"I guess we're both just a little curious about what's on the other side of the fence," she murmured to the horse. "That's all."

He whickered softly, as if he agreed.

Emma laughed and her feelings dropped back into their usual place, like always, so that she appreciated the cool breeze after all her running around, and the warmth of the wintry sunshine on her face, and the scent of the sweet hay waiting for Clifford in the barn.

She was tired. That was all. They hadn't been able to hire enough hands to help with the harvest this fall, which meant more hours for her and her brothers, she would feel better if she could catch up on her sleep.

Everything was still just right with her world.

Once she got the horses squared away, she headed over to her brother's house, where she found him on the back porch with a pile of wood.

"I'm working on it," Ansel told Emma before she even had a chance to ask about the fence repairs. "But it's tough without being able to lay hands on decent supplies. That idiot must be putting a fence around half of Tarker County."

She rolled her eyes at the thought of it, and didn't need to ask who he was talking about.

Sebastian Radcliffe.

That same idiot was the reason they hadn't been able to hire help this fall. The man had come sweeping in from the city and started buying up farms like he was starting a one-man land rush. And as far as she knew, no one in town had even laid eyes on the guy.

"Need anything from town?" she asked her brother. "I've got to swing over to the feed shop."

"No thanks," Ansel said. "I'll have the fence put back together by the time you come back, hopefully."

"Is that from the castle?" Emma asked, looking more closely at the wood piled up on Ansel's back porch.

It wasn't a real castle, but one of the old houses on the homestead had a black and white marble entry and even a ballroom, so they had taken to calling it the castle as kids. Unfortunately, it also had a bog in the basement, and tarps over a couple of the ornate rooflines.

"I doubt anyone will miss the rabbit hutches," Ansel said, shrugging. "And it's better than taking the doors off the ballroom."

When she was little, Emma had dreamed of restoring

the castle when she grew up, and painting every inch of it gold and pink, including the ballroom.

She still daydreamed about it, honestly. But she figured she could spare the rabbit hutches. It was only a dream, anyway. The reality was that many of the buildings on the homestead were falling to ruin, and they weren't going to find the money to restore them anytime soon. There hadn't been enough kids in the Williams family to work the land to its fullest extent in generations.

"See you," she told her brother as she turned to go.

"Wouldn't want to *be* you," he sing-songed after her like he always did, making her smile.

She gave him a quick wave as she hopped into her dad's old pick-up truck.

Alistair Williams didn't work the farm anymore. He'd been able to retire at last when Emma, the baby of the family, decided to get right to work instead of heading off to college.

He had a little sedan that was better on gas now, and he used it when he and her mom headed into town these days. The truck was still his on paper, but he had all but given it to Emma.

She strapped in and turned on the radio before taking the bumpy gravel road back up to the big house and the paved, tree-lined drive that would carry her to the main road.

The weatherman was on, trying to make predictions about what kind of winter they would have, and then the deejay announced it was Beatles Day and put on "Here Comes the Sun."

Emma hit the main road and headed to Cassidy Farm, trying not to feel too jealous when she pulled in ten minutes later and saw the beautifully kept property, the freshly painted octagonal barn, and the new glassy nursery they'd put in a few years back.

Cassidy Farm did well, in large part because they brought folks in locally for festivals and pick-your-own apples and pumpkins, and even cut-your-own Christmas trees. They'd had to hire a lot of outside people to work the shop and the nursery, but it had paid off for them.

She pulled through the public-facing part of the farm and continued past the *Private Property* sign to get to the big farmhouse.

Joe Cassidy was usually over at the feed shop, chewing the fat with Reggie Webb, another old farmer whose family had worked land in Tarker County for generations. But Emma knew Joe's knees were bad this year, and she hadn't seen him at the shop as often. She tried to make a habit of stopping by to see if she could grab anything for him on her trip to town.

"Emma Williams," Joe's wife, Alice, said warmly, waving to her from the porch.

"How do you always know I'm here?" Emma laughed, hopping out of the truck and heading up the front steps.

"Just a lucky guess," Alice said with a smile, wiping her hands on her apron and pulling Emma in for a big hug.

Emma let herself melt into Alice's arms for a moment.

Alice Cassidy was short and stout. She had ribbons of pretty silver in her chestnut hair now, but otherwise, she was just the same energetic and cheerful woman she had been when Emma was small and came over with her older siblings to play with the Cassidy kids from time to time.

"Come have a pumpkin muffin," Alice said, pulling back and leading Emma into the house. "They're fresh baked, and it's a new recipe. I'd love for you to try one."

Emma opened her mouth to say no, but the house smelled so delicious that she nodded instead.

"Thank you," she told Alice. "I've been chasing horses all morning, and a pumpkin muffin sounds amazing. But maybe I can take it with me? I've got to get over to the feed shop before Hal takes his lunch break."

"Of course," Alice told her. "Let me just wrap one up for you. Shane's in the kitchen. He stopped in to grab a bite. I'm sure he'd love to say hello."

"Great," Emma said, following her.

Shane Cassidy was older than she was, but she knew him well enough. He was a great guy, and he had two kids of his own now.

"What brings you here, Em?" Shane boomed from his seat at the kitchen island as Alice plucked a muffin out of the pan and started wrapping it up.

"I was heading over to the feed shop and wanted to know if I could pick anything up for you guys," she told him. "Then your mom mentioned pumpkin muffins, and my mouth started watering, and here we are."

Alice pressed a warm, foil-wrapped packet into her hands. It smelled like heaven.

"You're a lifesaver, Emma—" Shane began.

"No need," Joe Cassidy yelled from the family room. "I'm heading over there myself."

"Joseph Cassidy," Alice retorted. "Over my dead body will you leave that recliner. The doctor said you need to rest your knees."

"Let me walk you out," Shane offered quietly. "I can let you know what we need on the way. We really appreciate your help."

"Thank you again for the muffin, Mrs. Cassidy," Emma called on her way out. "See you later."

"See you later, Emma," Alice yelled back.

"She's a good kid," Joe was saying quietly to Alice as they passed the doorway. "Knows her way around a paddock."

Shane winked at Emma, and she couldn't help but smile. Once they got to the porch he fished his phone out of his pocket and texted her a short list of items they needed.

"Thanks again for doing this," he said handing her a couple of bills. "It's been a madhouse around here. I can't get seasonal help to save my life."

"We couldn't either," Emma said, shaking her head sadly. "At least our season is wrapped up, except for the animals. You guys go all year."

"Thank goodness my dad hired full-time workers for the nursery and the shops years ago," Shane said. "Those folks are as loyal as they come and grateful for the steady work. But I need seasonal help with the animals this winter more than ever, now that Dad is laid up. And I can't find anyone at all."

Emma nodded, figuring she already knew the reason for that.

"I hate to talk bad about any man, especially behind his back," Shane said, confirming her suspicions. "But that Radcliffe guy's not doing anyone around here any favors."

Emma shook her head. There was nothing more to say.

"Well, thanks again," Shane said. "Hopefully, I'll be able to return the favor one day soon."

"No need," she told him with a smile. "I'll be back in a bit."

She jogged down the porch steps with her warm muffin cradled in one hand and got back in the truck.

By the time Emma pulled out, Alice Cassidy had joined her son on the porch, and they were both waving goodbye in the rearview mirror as Emma headed back up the drive.

2

EMMA

Emma pulled into the lot at the feed shop, making sure to get a spot close to the side door to make it easier for the shop boy to carry her things out.

"Hey, Emma," a friend from high school called, waving to her as he headed to his truck.

She waved back and chuckled, glad she was running into people at the feed shop parking lot, and not the mall up on Route 1.

She was wearing the fleece-lined flannel her dad had given her last Christmas, along with a pair of jeans that were muddy up to the knees, and a pair of equally muddy boots. Her hair was in a messy ponytail, and she was pretty sure she was still red-cheeked and sweating in spite of the cold.

In short, she looked like she had just spent the morning chasing horses and checking the fence line to find the place they had escaped from.

But everyone else here had spent their morning knee-deep in mucking and feeding and the same types of tasks, so she would fit right in. And there was a coffee pot at the counter, where a little caffeine and farm talk awaited her. If there was a better place in town to hang out, Emma couldn't imagine what it could be.

She headed in and gave Sal her list right away. Luck was with her, and he confirmed that they had nearly everything she and Shane Cassidy needed.

He rung up her two lists separately and let her know the shop boy was loading up in the order lists were received and paid, as usual, and invited her to swing over to the counter to enjoy a free cup of coffee while she waited.

She didn't have to be invited twice.

"Emma Williams," Reggie Webb said happily stepping back to make room for her at the counter. "How's the farm life treating you?"

"Not too bad," she said. "Spent a little time chasing the horses this morning."

"Old Cliffy gave you a run for your money, did he?" Reggie laughed.

"Nah, he was a prince," she laughed. "But Violet and Duke were hard to catch. We've got rotten wood in the fences in more than one spot. I'll be in shape to run a marathon if we make it through the winter."

"Can't find anywhere for split rail?" Doug Arnold asked her.

"Nope," she said, shaking her head. "Dad's got a friend out in Amish country, but even he's cleaned out. My brother's home patching it up as best he can with wood from some of the old rabbit hutches, but that won't last."

Reggie poured a cup of hot coffee and handed it to her.

"Thanks," she said, raising it as if in a toast to her friends.

The men all chuckled and she felt a familiar warmth in her chest.

There weren't too many young women who worked the

farm like she did these days, but these guys had taken her under their wing from the first time she showed up here as a nervous teenager, encouraging her to come over to the counter and listen to them talk shop.

Once she got a little more comfortable, she had begun peppering everyone with endless questions. The seasoned farmers had been good-humored with her and answered patiently, and she'd learned so much.

Now, she was able to answer a question or two herself from time to time, and that felt really good. They all shared a love of the land that went beyond age and gender. Here at the feed shop, Emma really felt that she was among her people.

"That fancy rancher really pulled a number on us," Reggie said, shaking his head as though he wasn't bringing up his favorite topic. "Can't get help, can't get supplies."

A couple other guys joined in the lament.

Normally, Emma steered clear of the whole mess. After all, there was no point talking about negative things that they couldn't change. They might as well be complaining about the weather.

But today, after spending her morning chasing horses and watching her brother tear the house apart to mend the fence, then seeing the ever-positive Shane Cassidy being kept from his kids because he couldn't get help, she got sucked in, in spite of herself.

"He's not even using the guys he's got," she heard herself say flatly.

The whole group stopped talking and turned to her. They knew she wasn't a complainer.

"What do you mean?" Reggie asked.

"He bought all this land, hired all these guys, and he's got them all fixing fences and painting barns," she said. "But

I heard from a few of them that he doesn't really seem to know what he's doing or have an actual plan. So it's all just busywork."

Just then, a man came around the corner of the nearest aisle, and moved closer to the counter.

He wore a cowboy hat, a pair of boots, blue jeans, and a flannel, like many of the others. But there was something not quite right about the look. It took Emma a second to realize it was that every single piece of his clothing looked brand-new. He didn't even have dust on his boots from the parking lot, let alone the mud and wear of an honest day's work.

Emma had definitely never seen him before. She would have remembered. Even with the weirdly clean clothing, he was probably the handsomest man she had ever seen—tall with broad shoulders, dark hair, a five o'clock shadow, and piercing blue eyes.

She closed her mouth and turned her eyes back to the cup of steaming coffee in her hands.

"You all are talking about Whispering Ridge," he said. "Right?"

There was some mumbling and shifting of weight on feet, but no one answered him.

"Can I talk to you, Miss?" he asked with quiet intensity.

Emma had no choice but to look up. She was the only woman at the counter. She met his eye and arched a brow at him, willing herself not to blush.

"Walk with me?" he asked.

"No thanks," she replied.

"You clearly know a lot about farming," he said. "Whispering Ridge is looking for experienced help. You should come up and see about a job."

He held out a card.

"I don't think so," she said coldly, turning back to her friends.

Inside, she was boiling over. They had just been talking about how the small farms were struggling for lack of good help, and Sebastian Radcliffe was sending his people down to town to try and poach workers at the feed shop? It was unbelievably brash, and frankly heartless.

"Emma," Sal called out, waving to her that her order was loaded.

"See you later, guys," she said to her friends.

They raised their coffees in salute as she headed outside.

The cold air felt good on her heated cheeks, and she took a nice deep breath and let it out slowly. There was no point letting this kind of thing ruin her day.

"Hey," a deep voice said, just as she reached her truck.

"You followed me?" she asked in exasperation as she turned back to see Mr. Blue Eyes right behind her.

It's not his fault, she tried to tell herself. *Don't take it out on him. He just works for the guy. It's probably an awful job.*

"Listen, it sounds like you really know what you're doing," he said. "And these offers are very generous. Surely, you could use some extra cash."

He was looking at her ancient truck, and the unspoken implication that she must wish for something better made her want to slap him across the face.

But she wouldn't give him the satisfaction.

"I'm doing just fine," she told him, holding her head up high and not letting him see that he'd gotten to her.

"Which means you're very good at what you do," the man said with a warm smile.

She blinked at him, wishing he wasn't so dreadfully handsome. It would be easier to keep her composure. She would have walked away by now, if it didn't feel like something was holding her in place.

"What if you could name your salary?" he asked gently. "That would have to at least be worth considering."

Suddenly, she was picturing the Williams Homestead, and all the buildings on it with deferred maintenance. Could she name an amount high enough to get her started restoring the beloved homestead her family had lived on for generations? Or was she just going to turn her nose up at a possible way to keep some corner of the historic property from falling to wrack and ruin?

He extended the card to her again, this time keeping it low, so that if anyone came by they wouldn't see.

"I'll think about it," she said, taking the card before she could change her mind, her fingers brushing his as she did.

Emma felt a tingle of awareness slide down her spine at the warmth of his touch, and was immediately ashamed.

Just because he was handsome didn't mean she should be swooning. He was literally working for the enemy.

I need to get out more.

"Sorry I asked you in front of everyone the first time," he said softly, his voice a little husky. "I'm still learning the ropes. Hope to hear from you soon."

He was gone before she had a chance to react, leaving her standing alone in the parking lot, the card clutched in her hand.

She shoved it quickly into her pocket and got in the truck, wondering if she had fully lost her mind.

3

BAZ

Sebastian "Baz" Radcliffe was still thinking about the girl when he pulled into the drive at Whispering Ridge.

He wasn't entirely sure why he was thinking about her. She was young, too young really. And she was caked with mud.

His interest was purely professional, he reminded himself.

It had been shocking to hear what sounded like a young woman's voice at the coffee counter from where he'd been lurking in the pet food aisle. He'd come around the corner expecting to find someone much older than they sounded.

Instead, the slip of a girl was right at the center of the counter, commanding the attention of every grizzled farmer in the place.

Maybe all that muck had given her street credibility with the group, but he doubted it. She wasn't yelling or anything, but every eye was on her, and chins were nodding up and down at every word she said.

Baz's team had brought in plenty of new hires at the

various farming haunts in town. Times were tough, so all they usually had to do was quietly mention that salaries at Whispering Ridge were generous and the target took the bait.

And while Baz had explored town a bit, paying for his purchases in cash so as to avoid anyone knowing who he was and glaring at him, he had never done any recruiting on his own before.

But the girl was obviously something special, and he needed the help of someone who wasn't afraid to speak their mind.

He'd encouraged his team never to make an offer openly once it became clear there was some resentment in town over Whispering Ridge. Most folks would grant a stranger a word in private.

But Baz had been so eager to get the girl on board that he'd gone ahead and said his piece right in front of the others when she refused to walk with him. It wasn't like him to let emotions come into play in a business conversation.

And her defiant reaction was frustrating, but he couldn't help but admire her for it.

He almost felt bad for following her out and getting her to think about something that was clearly against her convictions.

Then he remembered his hand brushing against hers, and he stopped caring about the farm, the mud, and even her fury.

In that moment, he'd felt like a kid again, with wonder coursing through his veins at her light touch.

She's too young, he reminded himself. *Also, she hates you. They all do.*

He parked his truck and headed in the front door of the

pretty farmhouse. Naturally, Valentina was waiting right at the door.

"Any luck, Mr. Radcliffe?" she asked crisply. "Did the clothes help?"

Valentina Jimenez was all business. She had been his assistant in the city for two years already when he brought her out here. She was incredibly smart, a Wharton graduate from a working-class background, just like Baz. They understood each other, and he was fond of saying that she was the best hire he had ever made.

But he could tell she was unhappy out here in the country. Maybe he'd made a mistake bringing her to Whispering Ridge. She was still being paid the same, but she was basically just running the house for him now, instead of negotiating contracts and networking with the movers and shakers. He'd offered to introduce her to some of his friends so that she could find another position in the business world. But she had refused.

He wondered if she was cursing her loyalty now. Maybe she hadn't thought he would actually go through with this.

"I don't know," he said, shrugging. "They seem like what everyone else was wearing, but they all still looked at me like I was from Mars."

"The clothes are exactly right," she told him. "I did my research."

"I know you did," he told her. "It's a small town and I'm an unfamiliar face. That's all."

"Larry Bryce called again," Valentina told him.

"That's fine," he said lightly. "Is Weston upstairs?"

"He's doing his homework," Valentina said, nodding.

Baz nodded to her and jogged up the stairs to find his son.

Putting Valentina in charge of Weston's distance

schooling had been one of Baz's better moves since coming out here. She was an absolute drill sergeant, and the boy's progress was much better than it had been at the cushy private school in the city.

"Hey, son," he said, tapping lightly on the door as he pushed it open.

"Did you call the people about the internet?" Weston asked immediately.

Baz gazed at the miniature version of himself for a moment, taking in the slightly-too-long, dark hair and cerulean blue eyes that gazed back at him accusingly.

If he had to be honest with himself, he was just as demanding as the boy.

But where Baz was up before five every morning to exercise and get the jump on his day, Weston was low energy and insolent lately. He was approaching his teen years. Baz knew it was a challenging time, but it could still be frustrating.

"What do you need the internet for?" he asked. "Go outside, explore, enjoy this place."

He winced before Weston even had a chance to roll his eyes. It was exactly the same kind of thing his dad would have said to him back in the day.

"Sorry about that," he said, sighing and sitting on the edge of Weston's bed so that he was beside the desk where the boy sat, and more at his level. "I know it's important to you to stay in touch with your old friends. Yes, I have a call in with the company that does the internet."

"This place is ridiculous," Weston said. "The chickens are waking me up all night."

"Roosters," Baz corrected him. "Sorry."

"I thought they only crowed in the morning," Weston complained.

"Yeah, it's like that on TV, isn't it?" Baz mused. "But it's nice having fresh eggs every day, and fresh air, and a view of trees instead of buildings."

That sentiment was met with silence.

"Why are we really here?" Weston asked after a moment, leaning in. "Did you get in some kind of trouble?"

Baz stared at him speechless.

"Did you not pay your taxes?" Weston asked.

"What would make you think that?" Baz asked, feeling gobsmacked.

"Blake's dad didn't pay his taxes, and they had to move to Detroit or something," Weston said, shrugging.

"I definitely pay my taxes," Baz said, sighing. "We moved out here to have a better life, really. I promise."

Weston rolled his eyes and turned back to the schoolwork on his laptop.

"You're going to love it here," Baz told him. "Just give it a chance."

"Mr. Radcliffe," Valentina said from the doorway. "You have a call from the owner of the lake property. He's finally willing to hear you out."

"Sorry, son, I have to take this," Baz told Weston, hopping off the bed. "We'll talk again tonight."

But the boy didn't answer, and when Baz turned back from the doorway, he saw that Weston was staring at the laptop screen again, his pale skin looking almost blueish in its light.

He'll adapt, he told himself. *He just needs time.*

But he was starting to question his own decision to bring them both out here.

When Baz was a boy, he'd spent summers out here in Tarker County with his grandfather. They were the fondest memories of his childhood.

After losing his wife, he had yearned to give Weston something more than the city life he suddenly realized didn't feel like much of a life at all.

But maybe childhood was different these days.

He shook off the thought and jogged for the phone. That lake parcel was a gem, and the idea of securing it made his heart thunder.

4

EMMA

Emma paced her room, wondering what in the world she was thinking.

Her brand-new jeans made a swishing sound with every step, and she felt overdressed and underdressed all at once.

No one in the family knew it, but she had gone ahead and texted the guy from the feed shop.

She still didn't want to work for Sebastian Radcliffe, but she was curious to lay eyes on him, since it seemed no one else had. And she might as well hear him out, even if it was just to get an idea of what he was doing with all that land.

It's definitely not because his recruiter is so handsome...

She stopped and looked in the mirror again.

Emma worked on the farm every single day of her life, and her wardrobe reflected that.

It felt like maybe she ought to be dressed up for a job interview, but her options were either a church dress, or the dress she'd worn under her robe back on graduation day. Both options felt too fussy for the occasion. After all, she was going to be a farm hand, not a saleslady.

Instead, she had chosen her usual uniform of jeans and cowgirl boots, with a chambray shirt. She'd selected her newest jeans and the shirt she had gotten for her last birthday, and she had cleaned the boots until they shone.

In a last-ditch effort, she opened the little wooden box on her dresser and grabbed the pearl studs her mom had given her for Christmas the year she turned sixteen.

She looked like a more put-together version of her everyday self. It would have to do. After all, she didn't really want the job. And even if she did, he'd be hiring Emma Williams, not some city girl in a blazer. It was better for him to see her as she was.

She jogged down the stairs and grabbed her keys off the table by the door, hoping not to bump into anyone. But Logan must have been heading out just before her.

"Whoa, are you going on a date?" her older brother boomed from the window of his truck.

"No, I'm not going on a date," she said. "It's the middle of the day."

"Then why are you dressed up?" he asked.

"I'm not dressed up," she told him.

"Why are you wearing earrings?" he asked, his eyes narrowing in suspicion.

How was her rowdy, all-over-the-place brother all of a sudden Sherlock Holmes? He'd once forgotten where he'd parked his truck for a whole week.

She didn't have an answer for him, so instead she rolled her eyes and stalked away, hoping that her mysterious behavior might get written off because she was the only girl in the family, and the youngest. It wouldn't be the first time one of her brothers was confused by the behavior of a woman.

Once she was safely in her car, she took a deep breath,

and headed out. But the trip went too fast, and before she knew it, she was signaling and pulling into the long drive with the *Whispering Ridge* sign out front.

The sign was beautifully painted with gold leaf on the letters. It instantly made Emma feel out of her element, and her stomach began to tighten with nerves.

I have to see what's going on up here, she told herself. *If nothing else, I'll be the most popular person at the feed shop counter if I can tell them all what Sebastian Radcliffe looks like and what's going on at Whispering Ridge.*

She got to the top of the drive and saw the reason for part of the farm's name. A beautiful ridge stretched out at a distance behind the farmhouse. It was blue-green in contrast to the rest of the sepia-toned Pennsylvania fall landscape, because it was covered in evergreens.

A woman in a tailored black suit waved Emma toward a parking area beside the farmhouse. She parked quickly and hopped out before she could lose her nerve.

"Miss Emma Williams?" the woman asked.

"Yes," she replied, thinking it was funny to hear herself called that.

"I'm Valentina Jimenez, Mr. Radcliffe's assistant," the woman said. "I'll walk you in."

How many assistants did this guy have?

"Thank you," Emma said, getting closer and realizing the woman was younger than she had thought. "Do you like working here?"

Valentina looked surprised at the question.

"Mr. Radcliffe is a generous employer," she said, after a moment.

Well, Emma had known he paid handsomely already. What she really wanted to know was whether he was a towering jerk or not.

And Valentina's non-answer made it pretty clear that the real answer was a resounding *yes*.

She swallowed and tried not to overthink things. After all, she was only here to check it out, not to take a job.

Valentina opened the front door and escorted her inside.

It was an old Victorian farmhouse, much like the others in the area, though this one was pretty gigantic. With all the farms Radcliffe had bought, he'd certainly had his pick when it came to which house to work out of.

They headed through the foyer into a glassy addition on the side of the house. It looked like it had been put on by someone whose dream was to retire in Florida and spend their days looking out at the palm trees, but for whatever reason that hadn't been possible, so instead they had built a glass room that overlooked the farm they had toiled on all their life. It was impractical and drafty, with bare wood flooring to boot.

"Miss Williams is here," Valentina said, tapping on the door to a room that was hidden by some kind of shades.

Valentina beckoned to Emma.

Emma felt her pulse speed up, but took a deep breath and headed inside. Sleek modern furnishings filled the space, looking out of place against the country backdrop. She steeled herself and looked up at the man sitting behind the massive desk.

"Miss Williams," he said with a smile.

She sighed in relief at the sight of the recruiter from yesterday.

"I'll leave you to it," Valentina said, slipping out and closing the door behind her.

"Please, sit," the man told her. "I'm Baz."

He even had a cool name. She tried hard not to notice

how attractive he was, but it was impossible when his blue eyes glittered in the brilliant sunlight.

"Nice to meet you," she said, smiling and sitting in the chair opposite his. "This is an awfully big desk for an assistant."

He blinked at her, his air of confidence seemingly shaken.

"Not that you don't deserve it," she said quickly. "Recruiting for someone like Sebastian Radcliffe can't be easy in this town."

"Miss Williams," he said calmly. "I *am* Sebastian Radcliffe."

5

BAZ

Baz watched the girl's expression slide from friendliness into shock.

He probably could have told her who he was more graciously, but he'd been so blown away at seeing her cleaned up that he'd forgotten his entire plan and blurted out the truth immediately.

She was even lovelier than before, and his foolish heart flipped and flopped in his chest like he was some lovesick teenager.

Get it together, Radcliffe, he told himself. *You need her help.*

"I-I'm sorry," she stammered, looking anywhere but at him.

Baz knew it made him a scoundrel, but he couldn't bring himself to feel guilty about her discomfort.

Honesty was what he needed when it came to these land investments, and this was certainly an honest reaction. She wasn't trying to hide her emotions, and he was glad. It was more evidence that this young woman was exactly the kind of person he needed in his corner.

"I guess... I mean you definitely don't look like some

crusty old billionaire," she went on nervously, then caught herself and her eyes widened. "Oh. Oh, I didn't mean—"

"It's fine," he said, cutting her off mercifully and trying not to smile.

She had inadvertently told him that he was attractive. And now her cheeks were flushed, and she was even more beautiful than before.

Stop thinking like that.

"Sit," he told her, more harshly than he intended.

She immediately lowered herself to the chair opposite his desk, her lips pressed together like she was trying to ensure she couldn't stick her foot in her mouth again.

If he hadn't been so furious with himself, he might have chuckled.

"I'm glad you came," he told her honestly. "We could sit here all day and play get-to-know-each-other, but I think it's better to cut to the chase."

She nodded once, mouth still closed firmly.

"Good," he said. "You seem to have some strong opinions on my operation, and I'm curious about your ideas. What's your fee to consult?"

She stared at him like he was speaking another language.

He waited.

Years of negotiation had taught him that it was better to open by letting his opponent name their number. It allowed him to understand their mindset and put them in a position of weakness by asking for something.

And as an added benefit, the silence usually put them off balance.

"What are you talking about?" she asked him after a moment.

Everything about her manner suggested she really was

confused, and not trying to outmaneuver him. Was this really such a foreign concept?

He took her at her word, and sat back to explain.

"I want you to tell me how you think I should run this place," he told her patiently. "To do that, you'll need to familiarize yourself with every facet of the operation, analyze everything, draw your conclusions, and then walk me through your suggestions, step-by-step. A standard consultation agreement should cover it, unless you want to stick around and help with implementation."

She tilted her head slightly, as if she was trying to figure him out.

He waited again, willing himself to remain still as a statue, though he was longing to know what was going through her mind.

"You actually want this, don't you?" she asked at last.

"It's better than overhearing in town that I'm botching it, and not know why," he said, arching his brow, and hoping to get her to smile. If she smiled, she would relax. Then it would be easier to get her to hear him out.

Instead, she looked mortified.

"Mr. Radcliffe," she said. "I want you to know I don't make a habit of talking about a person behind their back. It's just that things have been a little more challenging for some of us since you got here. I was letting off steam, and I'm sorry you heard it."

"Make it up to me by accepting a consulting position," he suggested with a half-smile.

This time, she smiled back.

His heart pounded helplessly as he drank in the radiance of her smile. It went all the way to her merry brown eyes, and he suddenly felt like he would do almost anything to see that look again.

"I'm so sorry, Mr. Radcliffe—" she began.

"Baz," he corrected her.

"Baz," she echoed. "I don't really have time for consulting. I have my own family farm to run with my brothers."

He frowned, wondering why she had to get as muddy as a sow when she had brothers at home to do the dirty work.

"But," she went on, "I'll tell you for free that it feels like you don't have a plan here at all."

It took years of business experience to hide his surprise that she had nailed it with a single guess.

She was right. He didn't have a plan.

He had been working from a place of emotion instead of analysis, which was something he had never, ever done professionally. Until now.

"You need a plan," she told him firmly. "Just for example, you have people painting things that may need to be moved or torn down. And speaking of painting, you've hired most of the skilled day labor in the county and you're not bothering to put them on the right jobs. And worst of all, you're treating the land you bought like it's still ten farms, when you want it to be one."

"I need to make this worth your while," he said, leaning forward.

He was unwilling to play games anymore. She had grasped big picture issues without even walking around the land. Grossly overpaying her would still be a value compared to fumbling around without her.

He slid the pen from his pocket and jotted down a number on a slip of paper, then pushed it across the desk to her.

For a moment, he thought she wasn't even going to touch it.

Then she frowned and turned it over.

Her eyes widened.

"This is for a whole—?" she began.

"A month," he told her. "A whole month, and I won't budge on that. If I don't have you here long enough, I won't be able to formulate a detailed plan for a project this big."

She closed her mouth, eyes still fixed on the scrap of paper.

It hit him again how young she was, yet the weight of the world appeared to be on her shoulders as she looked at that number. She was seeing something in her mind's eye as she gazed at it, and it wasn't anything as frivolous as a shiny new truck, that much was clear.

"I know it may feel like a long time," he told her gently, allowing himself to break his business persona a second time. "But I also know this is a slow season in Pennsylvania. Can't your family get by without you for a single month?"

She frowned, and he could see that she was really imagining it, trying to picture her brothers doing whatever she had been doing to be knee deep in muck the other day.

"I'll think about it," she said at last.

"That's all I can ask," he told her.

She slipped the paper into her pocket, and it took all his discipline not to celebrate. He had been pretty sure that no one in her position could resist the number on that piece of paper. And she was showing her cards by not leaving the paper on the table. She wanted to keep it close to her.

It's not fair to negotiate with someone who doesn't know how, his conscience said suddenly, out of nowhere.

She glanced up at him, and he was transfixed by her dark brown eyes again.

"I should go," she told him, getting up awkwardly.

He stood automatically, like he had been taught to do as

a small boy, when a lady stood up. It wasn't a behavior that he usually carried over into his work environment.

He could have imagined it, but he thought he saw the ghost of a smile cross her lips as she left the room.

When he heard Valentina speak to her again, he strode over to the far window, which overlooked the parking area, to catch one last glimpse of Emma as she headed for her old truck.

The old clunker reminded him of his grandfather's beloved pickup back when Baz was a kid. The scars and rust never bothered him back then. He just thought it was cool Grandpa could fill the back with hay and drive the kids around the farm.

She had just reached the driver's side door when something caught her attention, causing her to turn and jog across the lot in the opposite direction.

Baz followed her gaze to where one of his workers was trying to lead a horse out of a trailer and it was giving him a hard time, as usual. He watched as Emma strode up, and the worker surrendered the rope to her.

She disappeared behind the door of the trailer and emerged a moment later, the horse following peacefully as she caressed its furry cheek. Once they were clear of the trailer, she handed over the lead and talked with the person for a few minutes.

Baz would have expected the mountain of a man to be angry that a young woman had done what he couldn't. Instead, the two seemed to be chatting away happily and even laughing.

The man eventually reached out and thumped Emma on the back, and she headed back to her truck, waving to him before she hopped in.

Baz watched the old truck until it disappeared down the drive.

Sighing, he began to pace his office.

Now that she was safely out of the room and he wasn't reacting to her pretty smile, he could see things plainly again.

She really was everything he needed.

He clenched his fists as he paced, tempted to text her and double his offer.

But he had a sudden instinct that throwing money around might make her respect him less instead of more, even though it would be the opposite for just about anyone else.

He would just have to wait and see.

It was supposed to be the easy part, but he had a feeling that this time around, the waiting would be nearly unbearable.

6

EMMA

Emma pulled out past the Whispering Ridge sign feeling oddly excited.

I'm not doing it, she reminded herself. *I just wanted to see what was going on up there.*

But she found herself strangely drawn to the idea, and it wasn't just the shocking number on the piece of paper in her pocket, which she had been certain was pay for a *year*, not a month.

Emma was the baby of the family, and the only girl. All her life, she'd been the weak one.

Help Emma. She's little.

Show your sister how to do it.

Emma, let your brother carry that!

It was only natural that her brothers coddled her a little and had maybe gotten stuck in the mindset of having to teach her things. But Sebastian Radcliffe treated her like an expert. He wanted her to show *him* the ropes.

Emma had never realized she craved the feeling of being able to teach and guide someone else. But after a lifetime of being the baby, the idea of a job where someone would ask her what to do instead of the other way around was incredibly seductive.

Of course, she still couldn't take him up on his offer. Even if it was the slow season, her family needed her. The homestead was already too much for three people to work alone. She would never leave her brothers in the lurch like that, much as she might like the idea of working for Sebastian—no, *Baz* Radcliffe.

She pictured his handsome face, and the way he had studied her as he leaned back in his chair, and a little shiver went down her spine.

He had no right being that attractive. And she stood by her conviction that he was too young to be so wealthy. She remembered how she had blurted out that he wasn't a gross old billionaire and felt her cheeks grow warm all over again.

She'd had the opportunity to sit down with the fabled big-city rancher and tell him to his face what she thought of his two-bit operation. Instead, like some desperate country bumpkin, she had essentially told him he was hot.

And it wasn't like he didn't already know that. No man who looked like Baz Radcliffe would be in any doubt. He probably had women throwing themselves at him all day long.

She shook her head and turned onto the road that led to the Williams Homestead. Generations of the Williams family had lived on the massive collection of wooded acres and farmland. How could she think of abandoning it, even for a month?

She pictured her brother out on his back porch, tearing apart pieces of the estate to keep the horses in after stupid Baz Radcliffe had bought up all the split rail in the county, and scowled, wishing she had balled up that paper and thrown it back in Radcliffe's face.

He wants to know how to do better, her inner angel reminded her. *Are you any better than he is, if you're not willing to show him?*

She tried to picture telling that man what to do, and couldn't.

The commanding way he sat behind the desk, her sudden speechlessness in his presence, and even his ability to write something down on a piece of paper and rock her convictions all told her that no matter what Radcliffe said he wanted from her, he would always be in control. If she gave him her honest opinion on what he should do, would it even matter?

She pulled into the Williams Homestead and let the long drive with its sentry of sycamores soothe her senses.

Coming home always made Emma feel like herself. The world outside might be filled with strife and confusion, but here on the homestead, she knew up from down. And even when they were having a hard year, there was always food on the stove and a roof over her head.

I don't need that money, she told herself. *We'll have a good year and take care of repairs on our own.*

Content that she had made her decision, she parked the truck and headed inside. Chester, the tabby tomcat, was sitting on a chair in the foyer. He blinked at her and flicked his tail once in greeting.

"Hey, Chester," she said fondly on her way upstairs.

Once she had on her old clothing again and the earrings were back in their box, she would grab a cup of tea and chat with her mom. A talk with Annabelle Williams was the most comforting thing in the world, and would definitely help her feel even more at peace with her decision.

But as she reached the third floor, she heard noises.

"Hello?" she called out, confused.

She was basically the only one in the family who came all the way up to the third floor, since she was the only one with a room up here. There were also a couple of guest rooms, a bath with a clawfoot tub, and some storage, but they didn't have any guests right now.

"Oh, Emma," her mother called to her from one of the guest rooms.

She headed in and found her mother standing by the back wall, a bucket in her hand.

"I was bringing up a load of laundry for you," her mom said sadly. "And I heard a drip."

Emma gazed up at the plaster ceiling, which was blistered and discolored.

Some of the other houses on the homestead had tarps on the roofs due to leaks they couldn't afford to address. It was a sad idea, but the homestead was big, and with that many buildings, they couldn't replace all the roofing at once.

But the idea that her parents' beloved home, the big house at the end of the sycamore drive, was leaking made her stomach twist in knots. And her heart was broken when she saw the expression on her mother's face. Annabelle Williams looked like she was losing a loved one.

"We'll fix this," she assured her mother, pulling her phone out of her pocket.

Taking a deep breath, she tapped on the contact for Whispering Ridge, a number she now knew belonged to Baz Radcliffe himself.

EMMA

i'll do it

She was going to put the phone back in her pocket, but it buzzed again instantly.

WHISPERING RIDGE:

See you in the morning

7

EMMA

Emma jogged down the porch steps the next morning, more determined than ever that she was making the right decision.

And it had nothing to do with her brothers' fury at the breakfast table this morning, when she told them where she was going to be for the next month. In fairness, she hadn't mentioned the figure on the piece of paper that was now hidden in the top drawer of her desk. That might have changed their tune a bit.

But part of her was still afraid that she wasn't equal to the task of consulting, and that Radcliffe would figure it out and fire her before she could earn an amount she was certain would be enough to re-roof the house.

She'd been thinking yesterday that it was pay for a year, not a month, and even now she wondered if one of those zeroes had been a mistake.

Instead, she had simply told her family that he'd asked for her advice and that he was willing to pay a fair price for her time. Maybe at the end of a month, things would be better for everyone if she could get him to let loose a few of the extra hands and stop overbuying supplies.

Ansel had nodded quietly, as was his way. But she could tell by the tension around his mouth that there was a lot more he wanted to say. Ansel would be responsible for the horses on his own during her absence, and that meant he'd need to be home to care for them mornings *and* evenings, even though he had a child at home.

Logan, on the other hand, had made a big enough fuss for both of them. Barely glossing over the addition to his own workload, he'd stormed about how he wouldn't be able to face anyone in town anymore if they knew his baby sister had gone to work for Radcliffe.

"Imagine how I'll feel," she had joked weakly.

That only made him even more angry.

Her mother had put her foot down and said not another word would be spoken at her table this morning, and somehow, even though she was trying to put a roof on the house, Emma had finished the meal feeling more like a rebellious teenager than usual.

It wasn't exactly the best mind frame for starting a new job, but at least she was happy to leave the homestead.

"Emma," her father called out to her just before she opened the door to the truck. "Hang on, sweetheart."

She turned to see him striding toward her and couldn't repress a smile.

Her dad's twinkly-eyed grin always made her feel more like herself. They'd had a special bond ever since she was small, and she knew how much pride he took in the fact that she wanted to work the family farm. This morning's announcement had probably hurt him more than anyone else, but he didn't look a bit unhappy.

"Emma," he said, wrapping a hand around her shoulder.

"I didn't want you to leave like that without knowing I'm proud of you."

"You are?" she asked, feeling stunned.

"I love that you work on the homestead. I couldn't have asked for a better compliment," he told her. "But it's important to spread your wings, at least a little. And if anyone can talk sense to that rancher, it's you."

"Why me?" she asked.

"Because you love farming," her father said simply. "And if you'll indulge your old man by listening to a bit of unsolicited advice, I'll tell you that it may not be easy to work for a man who is used to being told all his ideas are good. But when the going gets tough, you remember why you're there. You love farming, you love your hometown, and you want him to do better. It'll be easy for him to get offended by someone telling him what not to do. But I'll bet he can't help listening when you talk to him about what he could be doing, with your enthusiasm, with the *love* for the land and the animals and the people that I know is in your heart."

Emma felt tears prickling her eyes. Her father knew her through and through.

"I'll do my best, Dad," she told him, hugging him close.

"I know that, Emma," he laughed. "I don't think you can help doing your best. Now try not to worry your mother by coming home too late at night."

"I'll be home right on time," she told him. "She won't know the difference."

"Good," he told her. "I'm making chili tonight, and your mom is making cornbread. You won't want to miss it."

"Are you... celebrating my new job?" she asked.

"Might be," he said with a wink. "But don't tell your brothers."

She laughed and hopped into the truck, feeling much better about everything.

Emma pulled up into the Whispering Ridge parking area a few minutes later, but there was no one waiting for her today. She parked her car in the same place as yesterday and then headed inside.

The foyer was empty, and she stood there a moment, letting her eyes adjust to the dim light and trying to decide what to do. It probably made the most sense just to head back to the addition and knock on Baz's door, if Valentina wasn't here.

She was about to head that way when movement in the back of the foyer caught her eye.

She looked up to see a boy dart in the back door.

He looked to be maybe ten years old, but he wore a white button-down shirt tucked into a pair of gray trousers, and he looked *exactly* like a miniature version of Baz Radcliffe, down to the dark hair and piercing blue eyes.

"You're late," the boy said to her disapprovingly. "And you were supposed to come to the back door. Come on."

He moved as if to go back in the direction he had come from, obviously expecting her to follow.

"Um, sorry," Emma said automatically. "But I should probably talk to your dad. Is he around?"

And what about your mom?

She hadn't seen a ring on Baz's finger, but that didn't really mean anything. And it didn't matter anyway. Emma was here on business.

"No, no," the boy said dismissively. "I'm Weston. He told me that I'm in charge of bringing you around when you got here."

It wasn't what she'd been expecting, but this was clearly Baz's son, and he was obviously going to bring her to his dad.

It was actually pretty cute that he'd given the boy a job.

"Okay," she told him with a smile. "I'm Emma. Lead the way."

He headed out the back door and she followed, impressed that Radcliffe was doing something outside. He'd definitely given her a hands-off impression yesterday, but maybe he liked to get his hands dirty after all.

More likely he'll just walk me around, she told herself.

But when they stepped out the back door, Baz was nowhere to be found.

"This is where the fiber optic comes in," the boy said. "But it connects on top of the house somewhere, and that's the trouble. You guys keep saying we're connected, but we aren't."

"Oh," Emma said, realizing what was going on. "I'm not with the cable company. My name is Emma, I'm here to work for your dad."

The boy's face fell, and he looked completely crushed. In spite of his elegant clothing, he was still just a kid, and it looked like he might be about to cry.

Glancing around quickly for anything to distract him, Emma spotted a great climbing tree in the backyard.

"Hey," she said, pointing to the tree. "Maybe we can see the wires from up there."

"What are you talking about?" the boy asked.

"From the tree," she said. "If we climb the tree, we can probably see the top of the house."

"I never climbed a tree before," the boy said, suddenly sounding uncertain.

Emma swallowed back her surprise and gave him an encouraging smile.

"You'll love it," she told him. "Come on."

He scowled at the tree, deciding.

"Unless you don't care about those wires," she said lightly. "You could obviously just wait for the internet man to come. But they're pretty slow out here."

"I'll climb it," the boy decided.

She strode over to the tree and gave it a good look.

"What are you doing?" he asked her, predictably.

"You don't ever want to climb a tree that looks unhealthy," she told him. "And definitely you'd never climb one with a power line near it."

"How do you know if it's healthy?" he asked.

"Well, I'm mainly looking for signs that it isn't," she told him. "A lot of limbs on the ground around it, fungus, splits in the bark."

She was pleasantly surprised to see him walk around the tree, searching for everything she had listed.

"What do you think?" she asked him when he got back to her.

"I don't know what fungus looks like," he said. "But there aren't a lot of fallen sticks and there's no split in the bark."

"Fungus can be mushrooms on the trunk or rusty looking spots on the leaves," she told him. "I don't see anything like that, so I think we're safe."

"Okay," he said. "Now what?"

"We find a nice sturdy branch to pull ourselves up," she told him. "You only want to put your weight on strong limbs."

She chose a stout branch and climbed up, staying close to the trunk.

"Your turn," she told him.

This was the moment of truth. If he was scared of

heights, he probably wouldn't join her today, maybe not ever.

But when she pulled herself up to the next branch, she heard him moving behind her, and looked down to see him wrapping his hands around the branch and pulling himself off the ground.

His face was a study in concentration, it almost would have been funny how hard he was thinking about it, had she not known this was his first attempt to climb a tree, *ever*.

Finally, he swung his leg up over the branch and pulled himself all the way up. For a moment he just stood there, clinging to the trunk where she had been a few seconds before and panting, a look of triumph in his eyes.

"Nice," she said. "You're doing really well for your first time."

He grinned up at her.

"Ready to go a little higher?" she asked him.

He nodded, and she swung herself up a bit more, then turned to wait for him.

"Just don't look down," she advised him. "That's what my brothers taught me."

"Okay," he said.

It took him another minute to get his feet under him, but she was happy to see that he was being cautious. A good climber was daring *and* cautious.

"As we get higher, I'm being careful to only climb onto branches that are thicker than my arm," she told him. "And you're using the same ones I'm using, right?"

"Definitely," he told her.

She gave the branch she was on a good shake, causing the leaves to rustle.

"This would be a great branch for a tire swing," she remarked.

"Really?" he said, clearly awestruck by the idea.

The kid was a little breathless now, and she assumed it was excitement as much as the muscles he was using. They climbed on without as much talking and finally reached the apex of the thicker branches.

"Okay, this is it," she told him. "I'm going to move over, and you go to right where I am now. You should be able to see everything pretty well from here."

She climbed to the nearest branch and watched proudly as her daring protege scrambled up to the perfect perch to look over at the roof of the farmhouse.

"Now you can look down," she told him. "Just hold on tight to the trunk and try not to let yourself get disoriented."

She watched him take a deep breath and then look between his feet.

"Oh, wow," he said.

"Yeah," she said. "You made it a good ways for your first tree-climb."

His eyes met hers and he smiled like she had just handed him an award. She watched him as the breeze picked up and the branches begin to sway around them.

"It's nice up here, isn't it?" she asked, hoping to help him see it in a positive light. "It's like our own little world. Everything seems different from the top of a tree."

"We're not at the top," he pointed out.

"We're at the highest point that's safe to climb," she reminded him. "How thick is the branch you're standing on?"

"Thick as my arm," he said, nodding.

"Exactly," she told him. "As far as we're concerned, without any climbing equipment, this is the top."

He nodded and began to look around.

"Hey, look," he said, tilting his chin toward the nearest farmhouse. "That's the cable people over there."

Sure enough, the iconic white truck with the red lettering was parked by the house on the next farm.

"They must have gone to the wrong house," Emma agreed. "When we get down again, we can walk over there."

"Hey, we *did* figure it out from climbing the tree," the boy said, sounding awed. "They hooked up the fiber optic at the wrong house, and now they're checking the wrong house. But we can tell them to put it on the right house. *Yes!*"

She smiled at his happy yell. It was good for him to feel proud of himself for solving a problem on his own.

"You cracked the mystery," she agreed. "But we should head back down, so we can catch them before they go."

"Right," the boy said.

She expected him to be a little frightened. Down was always much scarier than up when it came to tree climbing. But he got that same determined expression on his face and lowered himself carefully to the branch below.

Impressed, she watched as he continued his descent.

He was nearly at the bottom when the back door swung open with a bang.

"*Weston*," an angry masculine voice shouted.

The boy jumped instead of lowering himself to the last branch. His fancy shirt caught on a stick on the way down and tore, but he managed to land in a crouch that was almost cool.

8

BAZ

Baz checked his watch for the second time, annoyed and surprised that Emma was late on her first day.

She had given him the impression of someone who was serious about work, in spite of her youth.

Maybe they did things in their own time on her farm, where she basically worked for family. But Sebastian Radcliffe expected all his projects to be treated professionally, whether they were in the city or out here in the sticks.

Launching himself out of his chair, he began to pace.

But when he reached the far window, he glanced out at the parking area and saw that her car was there.

Before he could draw any conclusions, he heard Weston yell from the back of the house. Sighing, he headed out back, hoping the boy wasn't yelling at the internet people.

He loved Weston more than life itself, but even he knew he had probably coddled the boy too much when his mother passed away. These days, Weston was addicted to his laptop and games. He didn't like going outside, and Baz was pretty sure the other kids at his elite private school in the city had him convinced that clothing, cars, and the trappings of money were what mattered most.

And Baz blamed himself for not getting him away from all that nonsense sooner.

Weston didn't even have a grandfather out in the country to take the boy fishing and camping in the summertime, like Baz had come to love when he was a kid. It would take him time to teach Weston to appreciate what he had learned as a boy, and how to relate to the new world he found himself in.

It's a marathon, not a sprint, he reminded himself. That was a quote from one of the parenting books he'd picked up recently.

The day he had come to his senses and realized there was an infinite amount of money in the world for him to chase, but only one Weston Radcliffe, he'd walked to the bookshop downtown and wandered into the Parenting section, buying anything that didn't seem to be abject nonsense.

That day had been the beginning of a chain of events that had led him here.

Opening the back door a little harder than he meant to, Baz looked around and didn't see anyone. But movement in the giant tree about a hundred feet from the house got his attention.

His heart stopped beating.

Weston was *in the tree.*

"Weston," Baz yelled, wondering what in the world had his indoors-y kid up a tree.

Weston jumped.

The whole world seemed to slide into slow motion as the boy dropped between the branches, a limb catching on his shirt and ripping it on his way down.

Please, God, please don't let him get hurt.

Miraculously, Weston landed in a crouch, absorbing the impact.

"What were you thinking?" Baz yelled as he ran for his son. "You could have broken both your legs. You could have *died.*"

Weston had just been looking up at his father, his eyes radiant with joy. But when he heard Baz's tone, his face fell, and he pulled at the ripped shirt.

"I wanted to see the top of the house," Weston said miserably. "So I would know if the internet wires were really hooked up."

"That was a very bad idea," Baz told him sternly. "You've never even climbed a tree before, and you picked *this one*?"

Leaves rustled in the branches above them and he looked up just in time to see Emma Williams scramble down, jumping from the same limb Weston had, and landing with the practiced grace of someone who'd climbed many a tree.

"Did you encourage this?" he demanded, feeling furious.

"I did," she said calmly. "It was my idea."

"Please walk down to the red barn on the left and have a look at what's going on there," he said through gritted teeth. "We'll talk about all of this over lunch."

She nodded once, her face a mask of calm that seemed to be covering an anger of her own. Though why she should be angry, he had no idea. She was the one who'd crossed a line by endangering his kid.

"See you later, Wes," she said to Weston.

"Bye, Emma," he replied, grinning at her back as she headed down the hill. "That's funny. She called me *Wes.*"

"Let's get your shirt changed before Valentina sees you,"

Baz said, turning back to the house. "You have classes online today, camera on, right?"

"Yes," Weston said. "But we have to go over and tell the cable people to come here. They're at the wrong house. We could see them all the way over there from up in the tree. The internet can barely handle a Zoom class. There's no way I can game online with it."

The boy pointed toward the farm next door.

They must have been up awfully high to be able to see that farmhouse. Baz repressed a shudder, not wanting to scare the boy.

"I'll deal with it," he told him. "Let's just get you ready for class."

"Hey, did you see me up in the tree?" Weston asked. "Or only the part where I jumped out?"

"I saw you land," Baz said wearily. "On your feet, thank goodness."

"Well, Emma taught me how to climb," Weston said. "And it's actually really easy. You just have to check the tree first, and make sure it's healthy. And then you make sure you never step on a branch that's not as big around as your arm."

So, the girl had actually taught him some safety rules. That was unexpected. But it still didn't explain why she was out back telling his kid to climb a tree instead of working.

"At first I thought she was one of the cable people," Weston laughed. "Can you believe it? I made her come outside with me. But she wasn't mad when she found out why, and she taught me how to climb trees. I'm glad she works here, Dad. She's nice."

The whole scenario finally unspooled at Baz's feet.

Emma had arrived, on time, and Weston had dragged her outside to look at the cable wires.

And when she realized his mistake, she hadn't gotten

annoyed with him, like most grown-ups would have. She had actually taken the time to show him how to do something wholesome and fun, at least in her world.

Weston had been outside just now, learning how to appreciate life in the country, in just the way Baz always wanted.

And Baz had reacted by getting angry.

"You should climb up there, Dad," Weston was saying. "You can see the whole farm from up there, and the mountains. And the road was like a snake. Did you even know the road curved like that?"

"That sounds amazing, son," Baz told him, meaning it.

When they reached Weston's room, Baz headed into the walk-in closet to grab the boy another button-down. There were so many of them, in so many pale, boring colors.

When Baz was a boy, he had owned exactly one button-down shirt, and it was saved for church and special occasions.

"I think I need some jeans and stuff for climbing trees," Weston said thoughtfully as he buttoned up his fresh shirt. "And definitely a different type of shirt. These are nice, but they rip too easily."

"Shoes, too," Baz agreed, looking down at the boy's scuffed leather oxfords. "But for now, how about we save the tree climbing for when there's an adult nearby?"

"Are you going to climb a tree with me?" Weston asked dubiously.

"Sure," Baz laughed. "I know how to climb a tree. I learned when I spent summers out this way with my grandpa."

"Cool," Weston said politely, obviously not believing him.

Had Baz really moved so far away from his roots that his own son didn't know him?

A storm of bad emotions swirled in his chest as he walked the boy to the little study they were using for an online classroom. Guilt and frustration were the easiest feelings to identify, but the pain of losing his wife, and the shame of not letting his son know his whole self swirled through it, too.

Valentina waited by the door.

"Ready for a great day?" she asked Weston.

"I already had one," he told her eagerly. "Did you know I can climb a tree?"

Baz nodded to Valentina and jogged back down the stairs to his office. But when he got there, he didn't feel like returning calls or crunching numbers.

I'm here. I'm trying to make things better, he reminded himself.

And Weston would forgive him for being awful this morning. The boy was a little whiny and a lot spoiled, but his heart was in the right place, and he loved his dad.

But Emma...

He tried to picture what he must have looked like, his face contorted with rage as he stormed at her for endangering his son.

That was enough to have him on his feet again, pacing the room.

He thought about heading down to the barn to apologize to her and make sure she stuck around, but there were a ton of guys down there, and everything would be ruined if he embarrassed her or himself in front of them.

No, the only thing to do was hope she stuck around until lunch, and then try to make things right as best he could.

He stopped pacing for a moment by one of the back

windows, and looked out at the big climbing tree instead, trying to picture Weston up in the higher branches, lit up with joy at seeing the farms and the mountains, and the road winding *like a snake*.

But all he could see was himself at the bottom, yelling at everyone.

9

EMMA

Emma stalked off to the red barn, wondering how she could already hate her boss when she hadn't even started working yet.

Had he really wanted to bring his kid out to the country, dress him like a nerd on a TV sitcom, and keep him indoors the whole time? Did he think that poor little boy was supposed to sit in front of a computer all day and never climb a tree?

If that was the case, Sebastian Radcliffe was a worse man than she had ever thought.

She walked on, and the cold November breeze felt good on her heated cheeks. After a while, the wide blue sky over the golden browns of the farm began to soothe her spirits.

At least I'm still working outdoors. He won't get me stuck in front of a laptop all day...

"Emma Williams," a familiar voice called out when she got to the barn.

"Daniel Sullivan," she yelled back, disappointed, but not surprised to see that the man had a paint roller in his hand.

Daniel was one of the best horse wranglers in the area. Yet somehow, Radcliffe had him painting the barn.

This is why I'm here, she reminded herself. *I'll tell Radcliffe he has to make this right.*

"What are you all up to?" she asked, looking around the barn.

There were quite a few familiar faces here, several hands who had worked on the Williams Homestead, and others she just knew from town and the feed shop.

None of them were qualified to be contractors.

"Boss man wanted a coat of paint on this thing," Daniel said, shrugging.

She scanned the barn.

It was ancient, and hadn't been well-maintained, but the location was decent if they wanted to use it for the main house at Whispering Ridge.

On the other hand, there had clearly been roof leaks. She headed over to the section Daniel was painting.

"Anyone have a screwdriver?" she asked.

No one did, but she spotted a rusty toolbox in the corner and headed over to find one.

"Your brothers must be sweating bullets," one of the guys teased lightly.

"They'll survive without me a while," she replied, grabbing a screwdriver triumphantly and heading back to the wall.

"But Emma Williams can't be stuck on paint duty," Doug Wallace said indignantly. "May as well have Leonardo DiCaprio painting the barn."

"I think you mean Da Vinci, and I'm not here for an art lesson," she laughed. "I'm just supposed to check things out today."

Somehow, in front of the guys she'd worked with all her

life, she couldn't bring herself to say she'd been brought in to consult. It sounded like she was too big for her britches or something. After all, in their eyes, she was still the baby of the Williams family.

The room went quiet as she headed over to the wall and stabbed the blade of the screwdriver at one of the beams.

She'd thought she was starting with a section of healthy wood frame, but the tool sank in like it was going into packing foam.

"Stop painting," she told them. "We've got termites."

"No kidding?" Daniel asked, jogging over. "How could you tell? There's no bugs. The wood looks perfect."

"The bugs are sleeping underground now," she told him. "And they're on the inside of the wood, not the outside. But they've hollowed it out here, and probably in a lot more places, too. They love wood when it gets wet. It's like ice cream for them. Can you paint an X over this support for me?"

He grabbed a brush and did as he was told, following her around the perimeter of the barn as she tested all the wood.

"How do you know so much about this?" he asked after a while.

"I grew up on the homestead," she said, shrugging. "We have too many old, wood-frame buildings to pay someone to inspect every year. So, we do our own searching every summer, and then bring in the guy from Kings every couple of years to be sure we didn't miss anything."

"Never thought about it that way," Daniel said, nodding with a respectful expression. "Guess that big old place makes you a little bit of an expert on everything."

"I never thought about it that way either," she told him.

"But I guess you're right, I've had to learn to do a bit of everything. Some of it by the seat of my pants."

He laughed, and suddenly she felt good about what she was doing here.

If Daniel Sullivan didn't think she was getting a big head just because she'd been asked to look in on things, then maybe the others would be okay with her new role, too.

By the time she'd finished two walls, her arm was getting tired, and most of the guys were sitting around. But she figured she was saving Radcliffe a few days of having a crew here painting, and maybe the barn would be salvageable if they could get someone in here to treat and repair it.

She and Daniel continued around the third wall, but when they got to the fourth, she heard a lot of feet shuffling and throats clearing.

She turned to see Radcliffe standing in the threshold with a sour look on his face, scanning his shiftless crew and his consultant putting holes in his barn.

"What are you doing, Williams?" he asked her calmly after a moment.

She almost fell over.

After this morning, she was certain he'd be screaming and yelling and dressing her down in front of everyone.

Instead, was calling her by her last name, like one of the guys, which would help her build respect with them. And his tone was neutral, maybe even curious.

"Exactly what you're paying me to do," she told him, in an equally calm voice, she hoped.

"Well, it's lunchtime," he told her. "Can you explain while you eat?"

"Sure," she said, wondering if she had inhaled too many paint fumes.

It wasn't possible for this man to have suddenly gotten hold of his temper in half a day, was it?

He nodded to her, and she gave the guys a quick wave before following him out. The bright sunlight outside had her blinking, but after a moment, her eyes adjusted, and she took in the beauty of the landscape. The honeyed gold of the fields contrasted with the ridge of blue-green mountains beyond.

"It's beautiful, isn't it?" Baz asked almost reverently.

She looked up at him, and saw nothing but raw honesty in his expression. She hadn't seen this side of him before.

"It is," she agreed. "Must be something after living in the city."

"That it is," he said, with a half-smile. "This way."

He led her right back to the tree where she had taught his son to climb this morning.

For a moment she wondered if he was taking her here to try and teach her some kind of horrible lesson. She didn't know many wealthy people, but books and movies sure made it seem like they could be very petty about stuff.

When she saw the picnic blanket laid out with delicious food, she almost laughed out loud.

"Hope you're hungry," he said. "I asked the cook for the works, and it looks like we got it."

"You didn't cook this yourself?" she teased, then immediately wondered if she had overstepped.

But he merely grinned at her and shook his head, looking almost boyish.

What is happening here?

"Have a seat, please," he told her. "I wanted to apologize for this morning. And I figured anyone who works as hard as you would probably be a person to apologize to with a good meal."

"I won't turn it down," she said, seating herself and taking in the sight of the delectable picnic.

There was crispy fried chicken, mashed potatoes, grilled squash, biscuits, and even an apple crisp.

Closing her eyes, she said a silent thanks over the meal.

When she opened them again, Baz was studying her with a thoughtful expression.

"Go on," he said. "Enjoy."

She took him at his word and grabbed a plate.

10

BAZ

Baz watched in awe as the young woman piled food on her plate like she was getting ready to hibernate for the winter.

He'd been on two or three dates since losing Ann. Though he'd taken them to nice restaurants, those women had all pretty much played with their food, either worrying about calories or worrying about what he would think.

This girl, on the other hand, obviously knew how to appreciate a good country meal. She was tucking in and moaning with appreciation on every other bite.

And he had noticed her pray quietly over her food, too. His grandfather had done the same, back in the day. Baz hadn't thought much about it since, but it felt like home to see someone truly thankful for their meal.

"You're not eating?" she asked after a moment, sounding scandalized.

"Sorry," he said. "I was just enjoying watching you dig in."

He grabbed a plate and put a couple of things on it.

Baz didn't work outside all day like Emma did, and

he'd had a big country breakfast. He was going to have to get back to a gym or cut back on all this if he wanted to stay fit.

I came out here to get back to nature, he reminded himself. *Getting outside to work was part of that idea.*

But somehow, he had gone right back to his city lifestyle, pacing on the phone and looking out the window at the only thing that had really changed—the view.

"You're not a big talker," she pointed out.

"Just have some stuff on my mind, that's all," he told her. "But I think you might be the key to cracking it. I'm glad you're here, Emma. Did you learn anything today that might help me?"

"Sure did," she told him. "But you won't like it."

"Try me," he said.

"I'm not even sure where to begin," she told him, shaking her head.

The movement reminded him of the electrician he'd met with this morning. The man had removed his hat and shook his head just like that before breaking the news that the entire farmhouse was running on old fashioned knob and tube wiring and had to be ripped half apart to make it right. He hadn't been able to look Baz in the eye when he delivered his verbal quote for the work.

"Money isn't a problem for me the way it is for most people," Baz told her as casually as he could. "Getting truthful advice is priceless though, and that's much harder to come by for someone like me."

"Well, buckle in, cowboy," she said, arching a brow. "Honesty isn't a problem for me, the way it is for most people."

"Hit me," he said, smiling at her gentle teasing.

"The barn that you have the guys painting is riddled

with termites," she said. "You need to get a good structural carpenter in here to deal with it."

"Okay," he said. "Wonder how long it will take to get one out here."

"Well, that's the good news," she told him, rolling her eyes. "The best structural carpenter in Tarker County already works for you."

"Why isn't he telling me about this?" Baz asked, wondering if the man was afraid of angering him.

"Because you have him risking his hands and livelihood moving horses in and out of trailers without any know-how," she said. "And before you panic about who should be handling the horses, you should probably know you have a top-notch horse wrangler here already, too. He's painting the barn."

"Oh," Baz said, feeling like an idiot. "Wow."

"Did you not ask these guys what they actually do?" Emma asked. "Or were you too busy poaching them to try and get the details?"

She closed her mouth quickly, as if remembering who she was talking to. But he liked her anger, it meant that, like him, she wanted things done properly.

"Believe it or not, you're the only person I actually hired myself," he told her. "The others were hired by my staff. And I'm not sure how they handled assignments, but obviously not the right way."

"Agreed," Emma said. "This is a major problem. Someone could get hurt. And in the meantime, you're not getting top value for your dollar. You just had five guys on a weeklong job covering up termite damage with paint."

"This sounds like an excellent first project for you," Baz decided. "Can you reassign my workers?"

"Sure," she told him. "But until you have a plan in place,

I'm just moving around the pieces on the board without a strategy."

He nodded, and looked down at the plate in his hands, wondering what he had gotten himself into.

"Why did you buy all this land?" she asked him softly.

He glanced up and met her pretty brown eyes.

She looked like she was actually curious, like if he just told her the truth, she could wave a magic wand and make everything turn out the way he wanted.

But that was impossible.

"I realized that being treated like a rich guy wasn't good for my son, or for myself," he said, deciding to show her one facet of the truth. "I wanted to simplify our lives. I used to spend summers out here at my grandpa's ranch. Looking back, I realize those were the best times of my childhood. I wanted Weston's whole life to be like my summers with my grandpa."

"Who was your grandfather?" she asked, sounding surprised.

"Elijah Davies," he told her, not expecting a reaction. The man had passed before she was born.

"Oh wow," she said, looking impressed. "Your people really are from here."

"No one would know it," he said, shrugging. "He was my mom's dad, so I don't have his name. And anyway, I've spent most of my life in the city."

"You should tell people, though," she told him gently. "It will make a difference to them."

"I shouldn't have to tell them," he said. "I should be able to make my own reputation out here without leaning on my grandpa's or cutting any other corners either."

She nodded slowly, something that looked like respect

in her eyes. He felt a flush of pleasure, like her respect made him some kind of superhero.

"*Dad, Dad,*" Weston yelled as he ran toward them. "*The internet guy is here.*"

The kid looked almost as radiant as when he'd finished climbing the tree this morning.

"I guess that's my cue to get back to work," Emma said with a wry smile. "Need me to clean this up?"

"Not on your life," Baz told her. "Go see Valentina. She'll give you a list of everyone we hired."

She gave him a funny little salute and jogged off for the house like she was light as air, though he had personally witnessed her eat enough to sink a ship.

"Hey, Emma," Weston call to her happily as they crossed paths. "Did you take my dad up the tree, too?"

"Not yet," she said, winking at Baz over her shoulder before she jogged away, her long, dark ponytail swishing back and forth as she moved. "Maybe you can try to get him up there."

Weston laughed.

And as Baz watched her move, a hopeful part of him that had been gone so long he hadn't known to miss it began to unfurl in his heart. Even her hair was dancing.

11

EMMA

Emma headed for the back door, feeling much better than she had this morning.

Whispering Ridge might be a mess, but at least the owner had a heart in his chest. If she could get him to make a real plan, he might just be in business.

He apologized, a little voice in the back of her head whispered.

It was odd to think that Baz making a mistake and telling her he was sincerely sorry would make her think better of him.

But somehow, it did.

Plenty of people were too proud for apologies, but in Emma's opinion, a willingness to apologize showed the ultimate confidence and strength.

She smiled, thinking about the beautiful meal, Baz's thoughtful answers to her questions, and the way he took her at her word when she told him there was a problem. She'd braced herself before telling him about the barn, but he hadn't even blinked.

Money isn't a problem for me the way it is for most people.

His words echoed in her mind, and she stopped to think about them. Had he only been patient because he didn't mind the expense of structural repairs to a barn?

Maybe.

But if that was true, then what was more impressive was that he hadn't gotten defensive when she had pointed out the issue with his employees being misused.

Like her dad had said, any man who had amassed a fortune like Baz's surely had a bevy of people ready to tell him all his ideas were good.

But he told her he had hired her to tell him the truth.

And he was as good as his word. The outcome of their conversation seemed to be that he was grateful for the info and eager for her to point him in the right direction.

Maybe he wasn't such an evil city billionaire after all...

Trying to repress a smile, she stepped inside and approached Valentina's desk.

"Hey," she said softly.

"Can I help you with something?" Valentina asked as she looked up from her laptop.

"I'd like the list of employees for Whispering Ridge, please," Emma told her.

"Why do you need that?" Valentina asked, her eyes narrowing slightly. "Mr. Radcliffe didn't tell me anything about it."

"You can absolutely ask him first," Emma told her, realizing belatedly that maybe the list also included personal information. "He wants me to reassign the workers to positions that reflect what they know how to do."

"It's not that simple," Valentina said. "Any shift in employment needs to go through Human Resources."

Emma started to giggle, then saw that Valentina was serious.

"You have an HR department here?" she asked, looking around like there might be a whole office complex she'd somehow missed.

"Of course not," Valentina told her. "I'll have to video conference with them—a separate meeting for each employee we want to move around."

That sounded like a lot.

"Why don't you just give me the list and I can make recommendations to Baz," Emma said, causing Valentina to arch a delicate brow at the use of their boss's first name. "He can talk with you about whether the changes are worth what it would take to implement. Sound fair?"

"You can make your recommendations directly to me," she said crisply. "I'm the liaison who will be coordinating everything with HR. It might seem simple to you to move someone, but the structure of a company is complicated."

"I'd feel better if you called Mr. Radcliffe before you give me the list," Emma said, deciding the woman was just giving her a hard time, and wanting to show her that she was open to her concerns.

"I'll obviously be calling him before I do anything," Valentina said, lifting her phone to her ear.

Emma would have given her some space to make the call, if there had been any space in the little alcove to give.

Instead, she had to pretend not to listen as Valentina told Baz that Emma had showed up in her office *demanding* the list.

The rest of the call was quieter, most likely because Baz was backing up everything Emma said.

"Fine," Valentina finally said, hanging up.

"Give me a moment to print it," she said, without even looking at Emma.

"Do you want me to come back later?" Emma asked. "Did you get lunch yet?"

"I'll have it for you in a minute," Valentina said.

Emma stood in the alcove, shifting her weight from one foot to the other, while the printer hummed. When it was finished, Valentina grabbed a clipboard and a nice silver pen and handed them over to Emma along with the list.

"I'll show it to you once I've got it all figured out," Emma told her. "Thank you for your help."

"Just show it to Mr. Radcliffe," Valentina said. "It will be his call."

It was clear to Emma that she had hurt Valentina's pride, but she couldn't think of a way to make it right in the moment.

I'll give it some thought, she promised herself.

She wasn't sure where she was supposed to set up shop with the list, but she definitely didn't want to stay in the little office alcove with someone who was clearly upset with her.

As she headed back outside, Emma couldn't help feeling that a cloud had passed over her sunny day.

She normally got along with just about everyone. It was hard to put her finger on what had gone wrong between her and Valentina. They had barely said two words to each other, and they were the only two young women on the farm, as far as Emma could see. She had hoped they might become friends.

I'll think of something.

She headed over to the picnic by the big tree that she and Weston had climbed together, just to think. Someone had already cleared the lunch away, leaving just the blanket.

Smiling at the idea of working out here in the fresh air, she curled up on the blanket to go over the list.

From the very first name on the very first line, she began

spotting talents that were being misused at Whispering Ridge.

Sighing, she clicked her pen and got to work.

By the time she had been at it for five minutes, the first page was a cobweb of crossed out names and notes.

And though she knew it would be a battle to get each of these employees moved around, she felt a deep sense of satisfaction that in spite of the ridiculous number on the piece of paper in her dresser back home, Baz Radcliffe might just get his money's worth out of her after all.

12

BAZ

Baz spent the day going from one call to the next, stopping only for a quick project in the house that he was actually feeling excited about, though the outcome was a little underwhelming, for today at least.

Suddenly, the sun was sinking, and he realized he hadn't checked in with his new consultant since lunchtime. He wondered if she had made any progress.

Valentina had seemed a little ticked off when she called him about Emma wanting the employee roster. He'd meant to get to the bottom of it, but like always, the day had gotten away from him. By now, Valentina and the rest of his employees would be gone for the evening.

He toyed with whether or not to text Emma, and then decided it was better to give her space. After all, she was a consultant, not an employee. She was allowed to do things her way, and he didn't want to make her think he was trying to micromanage.

Hopefully she was at home, enjoying her dinner and relaxing after her first day.

As he passed by the back window, he spotted something

under the big tree. The picnic blanket was still there, but there was something else as well. He stepped in for a closer look, but whatever it was, shadows made it too hard to really see.

Intrigued, he headed out the back door to investigate.

The cold breeze was swirling colorful leaves on the grass and his eyes were drawn, as ever, to the ridge of pines above.

As soon as he got close to the big tree, he saw what was there.

Emma sat between the thick roots on the picnic blanket. She leaned against the truck, concentrating fiercely on the marked-up papers in her hand. The last of the sun's fiery rays made the highlights in her dark hair shimmer and dance.

What was she doing out here in the cold?

She's used to working outside all day, a little voice in the back of his head reminded him.

He watched her for a moment, then felt guilty for it, like he was spying, even though they were both out in the open.

"Hey," he said softly, not wanting to startle her.

Her dark eyes lifted to meet his and she smiled up at him, the furrowed brow smoothing instantly.

"Hey," she replied.

"What are you still doing here?" he asked.

"Guess I was in the zone," she said, indicating the employee roster. "You have a lot of guys here, and a lot of jobs."

"I appreciate that, but I don't expect you to stay past five," he told her. "If a month isn't enough time to get me straightened out, then we'll make it two. For double the original fee, of course. But you have to have a life outside of work."

"Why do I have this feeling that rule doesn't apply to you?" she asked.

"I'm working on that," he laughed. "It's part of why I'm out here."

"Then why do I see you pacing on the phone in your office every time I look up from this list?"

She made a valid point.

"Look, it's quitting time for you and that's non-negotiable," he told her. "But there is one more thing I would still like to show you today, if you want to see it."

"Sure," she said with another happy smile, grabbing her things and scrambling up.

He wanted to offer her a hand, but something held him back.

There was a sort of magic in the twilight here with Emma, with the sun setting beyond the blue-green ridge, and no one but the two of them around to witness it. In the brilliant fire of the sinking sun, it was almost possible to believe that real life didn't matter, and that wild, wonderful things could happen.

"Come on," he said, shaking off his silly romantic notions. The poor girl was here for a job, not for him to moon over her in the twilight.

She followed him back into the house without comment.

When they reached the door to the basement, he stopped with his hand on the handle.

"I'm not a serial killer," he told her. "I promise."

"I wasn't worried at all until you said that," she laughed.

But she was only teasing, because she trailed him down the basement stairs fearlessly.

"It's not much," he told her. "Just a rec room with some office furniture, but it will do for now. I'm renovating one of the cottages on the property to make real office space, so depending how long you stay, you might end up in more official surroundings."

"This is for me?" she asked, sounding awed.

He felt a warm flush of pleasure at having pleased her with this temporary setup.

"It's better than sitting under a tree in the cold," he said. "And I'll be able to find you, when you're not in the field."

"I love it," she breathed, scanning the space.

He took it all in, wondering what it looked like in her eyes. There was literally a pool table in the middle of the enormous, finished basement, and the carpet had the wild geometrical shapes and colors of a 1980s arcade.

But he'd been able to get a desk and an ergonomic chair delivered for her, as well as a small table with a couple of chairs, a laptop and printer, and some other supplies.

She was moving among her new things, admiring the chair, picking up a jar of pens and smiling as she pulled one out and clicked it.

"I just wanted you to have your own workspace," he told her.

"What's this?" she asked, lifting up the paperweight.

He suddenly felt embarrassed, like she would think he was trying to show off by putting that on her desk. He hadn't really thought about it, he'd been using it himself as a paperweight for years.

"Just something to hold your papers down with," he told her gruffly. "You'll have a normal paperweight and a couple of other things I ordered online coming next week."

"You won regionals in track?" she asked, sounding almost awed.

"It was a long time ago," he told her.

"Still so cool," she told him. "I'm a runner too, at least I was back in school. I miss it, getting in that zone where you feel like you could fly."

He smiled, recognizing a kindred spirit.

"I still get out most mornings," he told her. "There's a nice trail here, if you ever want to check it out."

"I've love that," she told him with a big smile.

Suddenly, the air between them was humming with electricity.

Baz longed to hold Emma close, press his lips to hers, imbibe that irresistible smile and bask in her irrepressible happiness. Her energy would light him up like the sun and he would shine on her.

What are you doing, Radcliffe? She's too young, and she's working for you.

"I, uh, should check on Weston's dinner," he said, clearing his throat and stepping back before he did something he'd regret.

"Of course," she told him quickly, moving back toward the stairs. "I guess I need to get home, too, and make sure my mom doesn't need help with supper."

He felt a terrible pang of guilt. She still lived with her parents. He was a monster for wanting to kiss her.

"Hey," she said softly, turning back and looking up at him so that he had no choice but to meet her beautiful brown eyes again. "Thank you. I'm going to do everything I can to help you make this place work."

She turned back and jogged up the stairs before he could reply.

Baz stood there for a long time after the sound of her footsteps faded away, wondering why he had a lump in his throat.

13

BAZ

Baz enjoyed a delicious dinner of roasted chicken and vegetables with Weston, while the boy explained the plot of a complicated video game to him.

Maybe it was just that Baz wasn't all that interested in video games, but he kept finding himself picturing Emma sitting under that tree with her hair glimmering in the twilight.

He had to scold himself inwardly and refocus on the goblins, gold pieces, and heroes in Weston's game more than once before the meal was over.

When Mrs. Luckett cleared their plates and wished them a good night, there was nothing left to do but head upstairs with Weston for their nightly routine.

Baz knew that eventually Weston would decide he was *too big* to read with his dad at night. But he was really glad that day hadn't come yet. And he suspected he was being granted a little extra time because their lives were in flux, and in an unfamiliar place. Weston always craved routine.

"How many chapters tonight, Dad?" Weston asked, as usual.

"Just one," Baz replied, as he always did.

They were making their way slowly through *The Count of Monte Cristo*. The swashbuckling tale had been a favorite of Baz's in school. And although Weston was a little young for it, and Baz had to explain some things and skip over others, the boy hung on every word and begged for more at the end of every cliffhanger.

He curled up in the bed now and Baz crawled in to sit beside him, opening the book and finding their place from last night.

"This is nice, Dad," Weston said suddenly.

"What's nice?" Baz asked.

"Reading with you at night," Weston said.

"It's my favorite part of the day, buddy," Baz told him gently.

Weston leaned his head on Baz's shoulder.

Love shot through Baz, piercing his very soul. These moments with his son were precious. He hoped they would continue, and that even when he wasn't getting sleepy cuddles, he would still get to hear what was in Weston's heart.

This is why we came out here. So we could have this time together. And so my phone wouldn't ring from dinnertime until morning.

That was one good thing about the country life. He might get calls all afternoon as folks were wrapping up with chores. But there was some semblance of respect for business ending when the sun went down.

He read until his voice got tired, completely ignoring his own *just-one-chapter* rule, as always.

When he could feel Weston starting to drift beside him,

he carefully put the bookmark in his place and closed the tome.

"One more?" Weston whispered, without opening his eyes.

"Tomorrow night, buddy," Baz told him, tucking him in.

He gazed down at him for a long time, his heart filled with the dark-haired boy who looked so much like a miniature version of himself.

Let him have a happy life. Let the world be kind to him, and let him stay curious and passionate...

His phone buzzed in his pocket, surprising him. There weren't many people who had that number. And he sincerely hoped no one had leaked it to Larry Bryce. The man had been trying to get him on the office line all week, but Baz just wasn't ready to talk to him yet—not until he was sure that the pieces were in place.

He tiptoed out of the room, pulling the phone out as soon as he reached the hallway and checking the screen.

LEAH RADCLIFFE

HE SMILED to himself as he picked up.

"Hey, little sister," he said softly, heading for the stairs. "What's cracking?"

"I just wanted to check on Weston, but he isn't texting me back," she said.

"He's asleep," Baz laughed quietly, as he padded down the stairs.

According to Weston, Leah was the best aunt ever, and Baz had no reason to disagree. She had spent a lot of time with Weston when they were in the city. She never said it out loud, but he was pretty certain she was trying to help fill the gap Weston's mother had left.

And now that they were here, she made it her business to message Weston knock-knock jokes almost every day and ask him all about life on the farm.

Baz had a bedroom in the house all set up for her, and told her he'd be glad to buy her a farmhouse of her own if she wanted one. But Leah had always been fiercely independent, and she liked her city life.

"Well, you know I like to check in on him," she said. "He was pretty bummed out about the internet, until today."

"Right," Baz said, heading to the kitchen. "Well, we're on our way to getting fiber optic put in, as of this afternoon. The internet man was here for hours."

"That's not why he was happy," Leah laughed. "I heard about the tree. And I'm impressed, Baz. I can't believe you actually let him climb a tree."

It figured. She always teased Baz for being overprotective. But Weston was his responsibility, so of course he wanted to keep the boy safe.

"Right, the tree," he said, grabbing a pitcher of tea from the fridge. "Well, I hate to disappoint you, but I didn't let him climb it, that was my farming consultant."

"Ah," Leah said. "Then I assume I should be wishing your farming consultant the best of luck finding himself another gig?"

He looked helplessly around the old-fashioned kitchen, as if the ghost of one of the former occupants might be sitting at the banquet, ready to advise him on what to tell his sister.

But there was no one to help, so he opted for the truth.

"Uh, she's still working for me," he said, clearing his throat.

"*Really?*" Leah asked, sounding slightly awed. "She must be beautiful."

Her tone was teasing, but it hit too close to home.

"She's *young*," Baz replied with finality, grabbing a glass from the cupboard.

"How young?" Leah asked, ignoring his tone and digging for more info, as was always her way.

"Too young for us to discuss," he told her.

"Intriguing," she breathed.

"How's *your* dating life?" he asked her pointedly.

"Ouch," she replied cheerfully. "You win. Let's talk about work instead. I want to hear all about your farm empire."

"That's not really what I was trying to do here," he said.

"I know it's not," she agreed. "But it's what you *did* do. Seems like a lot for a person who says he's trying to simplify his life."

"Yeah," he said, sighing and rubbing the back of his neck. "Emma's trying to tell me the same thing."

"Emma, the consultant?" Leah asked, with a tinge of glee in her voice.

"Yes," he growled.

"I think I like her already," Leah said. "Has she gotten you up a tree yet?"

"That's exactly what Weston asked me," he laughed, shaking his head.

"Smart boy," Leah said affectionately.

14

EMMA

A few weeks later, Emma was driving home from work, a route that was starting to feel nearly as familiar as the trail to the stables on the homestead.

As usual, she'd been trying to beat the sun as it sank. But it was full dark, yet again, as she pulled into the drive between the sycamores and her home came into sight.

She was more than halfway through her agreed-upon month, and it was already clear she would have to extend to a second.

And since she certainly didn't want to stretch this out to three months, she was working so many hours that she always seemed to be late to dinner.

But it wasn't all bad. Working at Whispering Ridge was surprisingly satisfying. Baz hadn't shared a master plan with her yet, but she was making all the disparate parts of his organization operate more smoothly, and with far less waste and risk. And the workers on the farms were even more respectful of her, once they saw that she was trying to make things better.

She only wished she could win over Valentina, too. For no reason she could understand, the polished assistant didn't seem willing to recognize the importance of what Emma was doing.

But other than that disappointment, everything about her new job was a blessing.

Well, *almost* everything.

"Nice of you to join us," her brother Logan's voice boomed as she jogged into the dining room after quickly washing her hands.

"I'm so sorry," she said to everyone, meaning it.

Logan's resentment hurt, but she couldn't blame him. He and their brother Ansel were each shouldering half of the chores Emma had abandoned to work for Radcliffe.

And they didn't yet know that she was hoping to earn enough in a few months to pay for a new roof on their family home and maybe tackle some other major repairs that were badly needed around the farm.

Baz was constantly telling her that he would pay her that same staggering fee monthly for as long as it took for her to get him underway. He'd even offered an increase for a long-term stretch. But she couldn't leave her brothers to run the family farm indefinitely.

"I'm proud of you for working hard, Emma," her father said with a little smile. "I've always told all of you that you don't need to stay on the farm for me to be proud, and I stand by it."

Logan turned his attention back to his plate, but not before Emma caught his expression. And again, she could hardly blame him. He was only thinking the same thing she figured everyone else was thinking.

If you want to work on a farm, why isn't your own family's farm good enough?

But she didn't have the heart to tell any of them about the number on that piece of paper.

As well as things seemed to be going, she wasn't fully confident she could get Baz the results he was looking for. What if something went wrong and he didn't pay her full contract?

She sat and closed her eyes briefly in thanks over her meal and then dug in, almost moaning at the taste of the homemade mashed potatoes.

Conversation picked up again at the table, and she was able to ask her brothers things about the homestead that she wasn't privy to during their daily work sessions.

The boys teased her a bit, like always, but with Logan, there was still an edge to it. After they caught up a bit, their talk turned to the long days they would be putting in come springtime.

"Emma's still putting in long days now," Ansel said, giving her a sympathetic smile.

"Probably Radcliffe makes her stay late because he doesn't trust her to get her work done in the normal time," Logan scoffed.

It was the final straw.

"Obviously, he thinks I'm competent," Emma said, setting down her fork. "I'm the one he's paying to advise him."

"Yeah, maybe he thinks you're competent," Logan said. "Or maybe you're just the only one traitorous enough to try and tell him how to take over this county more efficiently."

Emma was on her feet, walking away from the table before he could take another breath.

"Emma," Ansel called after her.

But she was already in the foyer.

"Emma," her mother's voice said breathlessly as she

trotted after her to keep up. "He doesn't mean that. He misses you is all. We all do. It's no excuse, but please don't take it to heart."

"Baz *isn't* trying to take over the county," she said, wondering why she was defending him before she even defended herself.

"Even if he were, family is family," her mother declared. "And your brother should support you in whatever you do. I'm sure your father is telling him so right now. Please come back in. I made a peach cobbler for dessert."

Emma paused for a moment, trying not to be swayed by her favorite treat.

In that pause she heard Logan's voice again.

"How am I supposed to even show my face around town when everyone knows my baby sister is working for him?" he was demanding.

"I think you all should just have dinner without me from here on in," she told her mother. "I have too much work to do anyway."

She turned on her heel and managed to jog up the stairs before the hot tears began to slide down her cheeks.

You're just proving him right, she scolded herself. *You're crying like a baby.*

But Emma had spent too much time hero-worshipping her older brothers not to take it to heart when one of them was angry with her.

However, she wasn't about to quit over some hurt feelings. She was sure that she was doing the right thing, and that everyone would see that in the end.

Right now, though, it was awfully hard living two lives.

15

BAZ

Baz jogged down the steps to the basement in the darkness just before dawn.

He had been running almost every morning since coming out to the country. In the city, running had sometimes been a chore, but here with the fresh air and beautiful scenery, it was a pure pleasure.

Ducking into the closet at the bottom of the steps to grab a sweatshirt and a few other items, he glanced up at Emma's office, as he always did.

As usual, just the sight of her work area made him smile. Emma had posted some pictures that Weston had drawn for her on the wall behind her desk. The depictions of her with Weston standing in the middle of a tree weren't particularly skillfully done, but they were evidence, however meager, that his son had experienced some joy on the farm.

Another drawing showed Weston riding a horse, which was something Baz knew hadn't happened yet, but it probably should sometime very soon.

This morning, something was very different about Emma's workstation.

Emma was sleeping in her chair, her head rested on one arm that was draped over the desk, her hair cascading over the edge of the desk in a soft, dark waterfall.

He was moving toward her before he realized it, stopping just a few feet away.

There was something elegant in the way she slept. She looked not just young and beautiful, but also serene.

He smiled to himself as he realized that he had never seen her be completely *still* before. The woman was always in motion. Like Baz, she paced and wandered while on the phone, and even when he found her in the chair, it was always rolling on its little mat, or her hands were flying on the laptop keyboard or dancing a pen across paper with such urgency.

A pang of guilt went through him.

She was working so urgently because she wanted to finish her job here and be done with it, and him.

While he might live for their five-minute interactions every day, and Weston obviously thought she was the coolest person on the farm, all Emma wanted was to get back to her family.

He gazed down at that sweet young face, wondering how she could carry the weight of the world on her slender shoulders. A lock of chestnut hair slid over her cheek and he longed to push it back, but knew it would be a violation to touch her.

As if he had summoned her, Emma blinked awake.

He stepped back, feeling like a complete stalker.

"Hey, I guess you were working late and fell asleep," he said gently. "I was just down here to get my stuff from the closet."

"Oh, no," she moaned.

"It's okay," he told her. "But you really do need to go home earlier."

"I would, but I feel like I can't stretch this out any longer than necessary," she said, yawning. "I have to get back to my brothers. There are only three of us, and it's so much land. We were already overextended, and now I'm pushing my time here from one month to two…"

She trailed off, looking like she wanted to cry.

"It's okay," he told her. "They know you're working hard. And I'm assuming the pay you're earning here is a help, even if you can't be there."

She bit her lip, and her expression was unreadable.

"Well, I guess falling asleep here was for the best after all," she said after a moment. "I've been getting home kind of late, and I'm probably disturbing everyone's sleep."

"Look, if you want you can stay here," he offered suddenly. "I have a nice guest room upstairs that my little sister refuses to come and stay in. It's going completely to waste."

He saw the temptation in her eyes before her expression turned resolute.

"No," she said simply. "You have to have some separation between your work and your home. I can't impose on you and Wes like that."

He smiled at the nickname. Of course, Weston *loved* that Emma called him Wes. It was part of the special connection they seemed to have.

"It's not an imposition," he assured her.

"Why are you up so early?" she asked instead of taking him up on the offer.

"I was going to run," he told her. "I keep my stuff in the closet down here, so I don't have to wake anyone. I guess that didn't work out so well today. Hey, you wouldn't want to join me, would you?"

She had told him that she used to love running. It seemed like a nice way to get a little time with her without either of them being distracted by work.

"I don't have any clothes for running," she said, indicating her usual button down and jeans with cowgirl boots. "Speaking of which, I need to get home and change. And make sure my family hasn't filed a missing persons report. I'll see you in an hour or so."

She was up on her feet and scurrying up the stairs in a heartbeat, leaving nothing but the slight movement of the office chair to indicate she had ever been there.

Baz watched after her for a moment, thinking about ways to solve her problem.

The obvious solution was just to let her go. But by the time she'd been here a week, he'd known she was improving conditions for every single worker on the properties, maybe off them too. He couldn't dismiss her in good conscience.

And of course, rushing the job wouldn't help her or anyone else. Yet he was beginning to understand her bone-deep obligation to family, and how much it hurt her to feel that she was betraying her brothers.

Staying in his guest room really would help her wrap things up faster, since she wouldn't have to go back and forth. But she had been so adamantly opposed.

Maybe because she can sense you longing for her...

He pushed that thought away, ashamed. Maybe he appreciated her candor and her knowledge. Maybe he drank in her smiles like cold lemonade after a hard day of outside work. Maybe she made him feel alive as a man again, after a long time of not even noticing women. He did long to protect and cherish her, or even just hold her hand and hear about her day.

But that didn't mean he *wanted* to crave her time and attention. And it didn't mean he had ever let her see what he was feeling.

Baz was fighting this attraction with everything he had. Didn't that count for anything?

Sure, but you can't have her sleeping in the room down the hall from yours if you feel this way, even if you're trying to bury it, his better angels whispered to him.

An idea hit him, and suddenly he was smiling and nodding to himself.

He pulled out his phone and shot off a text to one of his guys, then headed out for his run.

I'll have a talk with her tonight, he told himself.

16

EMMA

Emma slipped out of the house, feeling grateful that it was still dark. What would people think if they saw her sneaking out of Baz's house in the morning, wearing the same clothes she'd been in last night?

Her mind unhelpfully showed her an unwanted image of Baz wrapping one of those big hands around her shoulder and drawing her in for a kiss so passionate it made her toes curl.

Her cheeks warmed at the thought, even as she tried to push it away.

Even if it was fun to imagine, a man like Sebastian Radcliffe obviously wouldn't be interested in a simple country girl like Emma Williams. He was wealthy, sophisticated, and unbelievably attractive. And his life was already dedicated to his son. If he ever wanted to marry again, it would be to someone else with a fancy education and a lot of money—someone closer to him in age and social standing, who could help Weston fit into that world.

She was afraid to ask him his exact age, but she assumed

he had to be in his early thirties. At twenty-four, she felt like she must seem very young to him in comparison.

He's also lived alone in the city, travelled, been married, and even raised a child, all on top of running his own business, her inner critic reminded her. *You finished high school in the same district where you started kindergarten, and stayed with your parents afterward to work the same farm you've been working since you learned how to walk.*

She was so distracted by her thoughts that she didn't notice someone in the parking area until it was too late to turn back.

Valentina Jimenez was heading away from her car. When she spotted Emma across the darkened lot, her eyes flashed with accusation, like she wanted to say something.

Emma braced herself.

But the elegant assistant merely flattened her lips into a straight line and marched up to the house, walking in the front door and shutting it behind her without a word.

Emma felt tears prickle her eyes.

She hadn't done anything wrong. She had merely fallen asleep over her work. Though it might look like something inappropriate was happening, Emma knew there was nothing.

But she couldn't exactly protest Valentina's accusation if she didn't say it out loud.

Emma hurried to her car, feeling like an idiot for falling asleep at work. Who did that?

Once she was safely in the truck, she contemplated calling her mom to let her know she was okay.

But her parents left their cell phones plugged in and turned off *for emergencies only*, so her only option was to wake everyone by calling the house phone.

She pulled out her cell just to see if they had called, but the screen stayed dark. The battery was dead.

Great.

She started the truck and pulled out of the parking area, figuring it was just as well. She would be home soon anyway.

The worst part of it all was waking up with Baz right there to see her. If only she could have woken up a few minutes earlier, she could have just slipped out without him knowing she had fallen asleep at her desk.

He had looked truly horrified at the idea that she hadn't made it home.

And if she was being honest, he had also looked extremely handsome.

She tried not to think about the way his sweats hung low around his hips and the t-shirt clung to his wide shoulders. He was sinfully gorgeous, and so muscular and athletic for a guy who seemed to spend all day on the phone.

Don't think about it, she reminded herself. *He's your boss.*

But what kind of boss hired someone, paid them as much as he was paying her, and didn't tell her what he actually wanted her to do?

She had expected that once he got to know and trust her, he would explain his plan for the land. Instead, he gave her bits and pieces about his wishes for Weston and his own childhood memories here, but no real direction for the farm.

Something was missing. Why had he come out here and started buying up land now? And why buy so much when he said he wanted to simplify?

As she drove under the canopy of bare branches, she thought about all the speculation among the farmers in town.

Some thought he was planning to build a single, massive operation, big enough to take a living away from the smaller farmers who were lucky enough to have deals with the baby food companies and frozen food brands.

Some thought he wanted to empty the county entirely, buying up every single farm. While others tried to find some kind of strategy behind the land he had chosen to scoop up so far. Those theories were always the most outrageous, even if there had to be truth to the idea that he had something in mind.

When Emma looked at it, she couldn't see a lot of rhyme or reason to his choices. He didn't even seem to be putting a lot of effort into buying adjoining properties. But she was sure that someone with his business background wouldn't buy land randomly. There had to be a pattern she wasn't seeing.

Turning into the Williams Homestead at last, she decided the same thing she did every time she tried to puzzle this out. She wasn't going to piece this together on her own. It was better to find a way to show Radcliffe he could trust her enough to explain it to her.

Her mother was flying down the porch steps before Emma was even out of the car.

"Where were you?" she demanded, her voice pitched higher than usual, eyes glistening with unshed tears. "Are you okay?"

"I'm so sorry, Mom," Emma said, her own tears threatening as soon as she saw her mother trying not to cry. "I fell asleep at my desk. And my phone was dead."

"Oh, Emma," her mother said in an admonishing tone.

But she pulled her in for a hard hug and Emma let herself relax in her mother's arms.

"The prodigal daughter returns," her father said with a faint smile from the doorway.

"I'm sorry, Dad," she said.

"Come on, let's get some breakfast in you, since you didn't have any dinner," her mother said, wrapping an arm around her shoulder.

It was early enough that she probably wouldn't bump into Logan or Ansel, so Emma nodded, her stomach giving a growl of agreement.

"We had an exciting night overall," her father told her as he poured the coffee. "Your mom popped upstairs to check your room in case you had slipped in quietly. She didn't find you, but she found the leak had spread. We put most of your things in bins for now. I can clear out the second-floor guest room for you, until we get the roof re-tarped. Guess we'll need to do the whole thing now, to be safe."

"It's probably coming in around the chimney," her mother said, setting down a big plate of bacon, eggs, and toast with jam in front of her. "Maybe just a little tar around the flashing would tide us over for a spell."

Emma's heart sank as she listened to her parents discuss all the ways they could push off the necessary job of replacing the roof of the old house.

It was one thing to have heard similar conversations over the last few years about the roofing on various empty houses and outbuildings on the homestead. But it broke her heart to hear them talk this way about the beloved house that had been home to her family for generations.

I have to complete this project and get paid, she told herself fiercely. *And I need to do it right, so he has to tell me what he wants.*

She looked up at her parents, who had always done

whatever it took to give Emma and her brothers everything they needed, and promised them silently that she would make this one thing happen for them, whatever it took.

I'll talk to him tonight, she decided.

17

EMMA

Later that morning, Emma headed back to her office from the barn, where she had been checking on the carpenter's assessment of the termite damage.

The sky was slate gray and the air tasted like snow, but nothing was coming down yet. That was a good thing, as an unusually early snowfall might slow down progress on the farms.

The other good thing was that no one had treated her differently today, made any knowing comments, or teased her about sleeping over with the boss.

In Emma's experience, farm hands were more gossipy than the ladies who lunched in the little café at the Co-op in town. If they weren't whispering about her, it could only mean one thing.

Valentina had kept her mouth shut about what she saw this morning.

Maybe it was because she trusted that Emma was not the type of woman to disgrace herself with her boss. Or maybe it was that she thought Emma was too much of a farm girl to get Baz's attention in that way.

But neither of those answers really fit. So, Emma chose to believe it was because Valentina was deliberately respecting the privacy of a fellow woman, whether she liked her on a personal level or not.

And that was a quality to admire.

Sisters before misters, Emma thought to herself as she headed down to her office, more determined than ever to win over Baz's cool-headed assistant.

She was concentrating so hard on this goal, that she didn't realize Wes was in the rec room until she almost bumped into him on the way to her desk.

"Oh," she said, jumping a little. "I didn't expect to see you."

"I'm sorry," he said, sounding a little dejected.

"I'm so glad you're here," she said quickly. "What has your day been like?"

Wes came down more and more often lately.

She knew he was lonely, so she always made a little time to hang out and chat, or tell him about something cool that was happening on the farm that he should check out.

"Boring," he said, sliding his hand along the surface of the ping pong table. "What is this thing?"

"It's a ping pong table," she said, trying not to chuckle. What kind of kid had never seen a ping pong table?

A really, really rich one, the voice in the back of her head reminded her.

She wondered yet again what it was like for him to go from what was undoubtedly an opulent city lifestyle to living in a massive, but old-fashioned country house.

He was definitely lonely here.

Money can't buy everything...

"Want to play?" she offered, forcing herself not to think about the folder full of info she had just gathered that needed to be entered into the system she'd created to keep track of projects.

"Sure," Wes said, still sounding down.

She grabbed the paddles and handed him one. When she gave him a rundown of the rules, he only nodded and headed to his side of the table.

"Hey," she said, following instead of going to her side to serve. "Do you want to tell me what's going on today? You seem really down. No judgement. I promise."

He didn't answer right away, but she waited, feeling certain he did want to talk about it.

"No judgement?" he asked after a moment, the blue eyes that were so like his father's pinned to her.

"Of course not," she told him.

He sighed and his eyes dropped to his paddle, which he was twisting nervously in his hands.

"I want to go back to the city," he said softly.

She nodded, but kept her mouth shut, hoping he would elaborate.

"But my dad is always saying how great this place is," he went on, after a moment. "And I... I just don't understand. It's so boring here. I just want to go home."

Her heart hurt for him, but she forced herself to remain as neutral as possible, so he would keep talking.

"Why?" she asked gently.

"There's nothing to do," he said flatly. "And I have no friends."

"Making friends takes time," she allowed. "But I do think you should talk to your dad and tell him how you feel."

He shrugged, but his expression told her he didn't want to do that.

"Are you worried he'll be mad at you?" she asked. "Or are you afraid of hurting his feelings?"

"I don't know," Wes said miserably. "Both?"

"If it helps, I think he would rather be angry or hurt or both than have you think you can't tell him about what you want or how you feel," she told him. "He loves you so much. If you're unhappy, he definitely wants to know about it."

Wes shrugged again, his eyes back on the paddle.

"Still want to play me?" she asked, smiling at him so he would know it was okay to share his feelings with *her*.

He nodded, giving her back the tiniest smile.

"I'll tell you what," she said. "If I beat you, will you talk to your dad?"

His expression turned serious, and then he nodded slowly.

"Great," she said and smiled at him warmly.

Emma didn't have a lot of experience with ping pong, but some had to be better than none. And she was pretty quick on her feet after wrangling farm animals all her life. She figured she could trounce this preppy kid in a heartbeat. Though of course she would give him a fighting chance and be sure not to embarrass him.

"Ready?" she asked him with a smile.

"I guess so," he shrugged.

She served the ball as slowly as possible, hoping he'd be able to hit it.

When he sent it back to her at lightning speed, she almost missed it entirely.

Reaching out with her paddle at the last possible moment, she managed to get it back over the center. But it landed on the floor, completely out of bounds, and bounced away.

"Whoa," Wes laughed, darting off to retrieve it.

"Guess I'm a little rusty," she admitted.

They continued their game, Wes impressing her at every turn.

"I thought you said you never played this before," she accused him with a big smile.

"I take tennis lessons at home," he laughed. "I guess it's kind of like that, but smaller and faster."

He still thinks of the city as home.

"I guess so," Emma panted, trying and failing to hit the ball back to him.

The game continued with Wes completely mopping the floor with her. His spirits were lifted though, and that was all that mattered.

Emma found herself cheering for him, even though at home with her brothers she was always incredibly competitive, and definitely a bit of a sore loser.

At last, he took the winning point and she pretended to fall down on the table and faint from exhaustion.

Wes howled with laughter.

"Well," she said, straightening up after a moment. "I guess you won, fair and square."

She offered him her hand and he took it and shook firmly. Emma didn't let go, and used her hold on his hand to pull him slightly closer so she could lean in.

"*I still think you should talk to your dad, though,*" she whispered, letting go afterward, and fixing him with a questioning look.

"Okay, fine," he laughed. "But if he gets mad at me, you have to play ping pong with me again tomorrow."

"That's fair, Wes," she agreed. "Though it's kind of weak

negotiation since I definitely want to play ping pong with you tomorrow anyway."

Wes laughed as he disappeared up the stairs and she felt a little wave of happiness wash over her.

She couldn't be doing too badly, if a kid like Wes came to her for advice.

18

BAZ

Baz sat outside with Weston, looking out at the sunset painting the farm in fiery colors.

They were both bundled up, wearing the knitted scarves Mrs. Luckett had surprised them with at suppertime. There was bite in the air tonight, and Baz swore it smelled like snow.

"I want to go home," Weston said so softly that Baz could have pretended he hadn't heard.

"Back to the house?" Baz asked him, knowing the real answer.

"I want to go back to our house in the city," Weston said, sadness pulling the end of the sentence up like a song. "I want to go home."

Baz froze, closing his eyes.

That home was the only one where Weston had lived with Ann, even if he barely remembered her. Baz knew that probably wasn't what the boy missed about it, but he did feel guilty for taking him farther from where they had all been together.

"What do you miss about it?" he asked, willing himself to stay calm.

"I miss school and my friends," Weston said. "I miss Chinese food and fast internet. And I miss walking to get ice cream with Dylan and Jayden. Kind of everything, I guess."

Baz took that in, making himself picture each of the things Weston mentioned.

"You went to that same school your whole life," he acknowledged, nodding. "And so did your friends. You had fun going places by yourself with kids you knew well, and you can't do that here yet. And we haven't found good Chinese food either, but that's my fault. I'll bet there's a great restaurant nearby. And, hey, if you want to invite one of your old friends out for the weekend, we could do that. You could show them all around the farm."

"You said when we came here we would do stuff," Weston said suddenly.

The vague complaint hit Baz in the chest.

"We'll be doing all kinds of stuff out here," Baz told him, wrapping an arm around his shoulder. "I just need to get this farm situation squared away, and then we'll pitch a tent and camp outside, just like I used to with Grandpa. We can light a bonfire and roast marshmallows, and I'll tell you scary stories."

Weston smiled, but the smile didn't reach his eyes.

"You will learn to love those things," Baz told him. "I promise. Even more than fast internet."

Weston nodded.

He was a good boy. He didn't understand yet, but soon he would. He'd never want to leave once this place got hold of his heart.

"Hey, Weston," Baz said, pulling the boy a little closer

and snuffling his hair, pretending to be a curious bear, like he did when the boy was small.

"Yeah, Dad?" Weston laughed.

"I'm really glad you came to talk to me about this," Baz told him. "I know that wasn't easy, you know how much I love this place."

"Yeah," Weston said.

"Tomorrow, we'll find Chinese food," Baz told him. "I miss it too. I think there's a place in the village. What do you say?"

"Sounds good," Weston said. "Can Emma come, too?"

Baz blinked back his surprise.

"Uh, sure," he said. "If she has time."

"She told me to talk to you," Weston said suddenly. "She said if I was unhappy, you'd want to know."

Suddenly, Baz had a lump in his throat, and he wasn't exactly sure why.

"She's a good friend to you, isn't she?" he asked Weston.

Weston nodded, his expression solemn.

"And she's right," Baz told him. "I do always want to know if you're unhappy."

"That's why we have to buy her a mountain of Chinese food," Weston cried, suddenly seeming more cheerful.

"I think she would like that," Baz chuckled, remembering Emma's enthusiasm for a good meal. "I'll talk to her tonight."

Weston leaned his head on Baz's shoulder, and for a long time they watched the sun go down in silence. After some time, a voice brought Baz out of his thoughts.

"Oh, there you are," Emma's voice carried to them as she walked across the lawn. "I was hoping to chat with you before you took off, Baz."

"Hi, Emma," Weston piped up.

"Wes, my goodness," she exclaimed. "I didn't even see you there in the shadows. Did you tell your dad about how you kicked my butt in ping pong today?"

Weston began to giggle.

"He did not," Baz said.

"He's too modest," Emma said. "Or maybe he's trying to save my dignity."

Weston was laughing his head off now.

"He really got you good, huh?" Baz asked.

"It was tragic," she confirmed sadly.

"I'm sorry, Emma," Weston said, popping up and running over to wrap an arm around her waist. "I'll teach you how to play better."

"Then maybe I can finally beat my brothers," she said, perking up and giving him a wink.

"I need to talk to Emma alone for a few minutes, Weston," Baz told the boy as he hopped up from the ground. "Why don't you head in and get your homework done?"

"Don't forget to tell her what we talked about," Weston said, pointing to his dad.

"Don't worry," Baz laughed, pointing back at him.

He watched the boy run for the house, feeling deep gratitude that at least the child was feeling better, for now.

"He's so awesome," Emma said.

"We had a bit of a heart-to-heart tonight," Baz told her. "Thanks to you, I hear."

She turned back to him, looking a little self-conscious.

"I'm grateful," he told her, clearing his throat. "You were right. I do want him to be able to tell me anything. It means the world to me that you told him I would want to be there for him."

"I know you do," she said simply. "You're doing all of this for him."

He nodded, trying to read the question in her eyes that she wasn't asking.

"Have you thought about putting him in school here?" she asked, after a moment. "So he can make some new friends?"

"I've thought about it," Baz allowed. "But it's a big adjustment. The online courses are on the same level as his old school. And I'm afraid if he feels like he doesn't fit in at school here, things might get worse. I wanted to let him adjust to one thing at a time."

She nodded thoughtfully, but she was still frowning.

"You disagree?" he asked.

"He's your son," she said, lifting her hands as if in surrender. "You know him best."

"But?" Baz asked.

"But I think he's lonely," she said after a moment, then brightened. "Speaking of that, can I bring my nephew over tomorrow? He's got a day off school, and maybe it would be nice for Wes to have another kid to hang out with, even though Lucas is a few years older. He's on the shy side, so it would be great for him too, I think."

"You're incredible," Baz heard himself say.

Her eyebrows went straight up.

"You come here and you just... fix things," he said, shaking his head.

"Not really," she said, getting a troubled look on her face again.

But that only reminded him of what he had originally been planning to talk with her about tonight.

"Listen, I can't fix everything either," he told her. "But I think I might be able to fix one thing. Can I show it to you?"

"Sure," she said, her eyes dancing with interest.

Emma loves a surprise, he realized, tucking the information away for later.

He led the way down the trail a bit, enjoying the friendly silence between them. The breeze picked up, lifting Emma's dark hair and trailing the scent of her shampoo to him. She worked so hard, and held her own with the guys, but the scent of her was so feminine that it almost made his knees buckle.

She caught him looking at her and smiled.

He smiled back, his heart pounding.

Stop thinking about her scent. Stop smiling at her.

But he couldn't. It was all he could do to keep his feet moving, and his mouth shut when he wanted so badly to take her hands, pull her close, and kiss her smiling lips.

They reached the little stone cottage on the edge of the woods just as the sun sank. Luckily, when he checked on the contractor's work earlier, he had thought to put the lights on inside. Now the windows glowed warmly, making the little house look as welcoming as a painting.

"What is this?" Emma asked softly, her eyes drinking in the pretty little house.

"It's yours," he told her simply, holding out a key. "Well, not like I'm just giving it to you. But for as long as you're here on the farms, you can work here, and live here too, if you want."

The key twinkled in the air between them.

"Really?" she breathed, looking like he was giving her the moon, rather than just use of a house that was already here.

"Of course," he told her. "I had it fixed up a bit, and there's some furniture—nothing fancy. But if there's anything else you need to feel comfortable, just let me know."

She took the key from his hand reverently, as if it were a magical thing that might disappear if she took it carelessly.

A shiver of lightning zapped down Baz's spine at her touch.

He had meant to just give her the key and then head back to the main house. But when she moved toward the door, he drifted after her, as if he were caught up in her wake.

Emma opened the door and stepped inside, letting out a little squeak of happiness. He followed, wondering what had delighted her.

She was spinning around in the tiny living room, arms spread wide, like she was in a field of daisies instead of a tiny cottage with low ceilings and lumpy plaster walls.

"There's a fireplace," she enthused. "And it has deep windowsills, and cozy furniture. And look. Look at that original woodwork."

He followed her to the fireplace, where she was examining the built-in cupboards on each side.

"This one is for kindling," she said, nodding to herself. "But the other one...?"

He opened it for her, revealing a little bookshelf inside, already stocked with some paperbacks he had picked up in town.

"Amazing," Emma sighed happily.

"I had them set up an office in the dining room space," he told her, indicating the other half of the open living area. "That way, you can work here during the day whenever you want, and no one will disturb you."

"Thank you," she said, straightening and heading over to check it out. "Oh, there's such a peaceful view from the table."

He joined her and saw that she was right. She had the

same view of the farm, with the ridge of evergreens behind it, that he had in his kitchen.

"And the kitchen is stocked," he told her, clearing his throat. "So, you can stay over starting tonight, if you want. And there's a bedroom and bath upstairs with fresh linens and whatever else we thought you might need. Again, just let me know if we missed anything."

"Baz, this is just…" she trailed off, shaking her head. She was sliding the key between her fingers nervously.

"I want you to feel at home," he said gently. "That's all. And hopefully, you'll feel more at home now that you have space of your own. Your work is important, and you spend enough hours here every day that it only makes sense for you to be more comfortable."

She nodded, biting her lip, and he had to clench his fists to stop himself from begging her to tell him what was wrong and how he could fix it.

"I'm just everyone's baby sister at home," she said quietly, looking down at the key in her hand as she slid it between her fingers. "It doesn't even feel real to me that anyone would value my work enough to do something like this."

Fury raged in his heart that this brilliant woman would ever be treated as anything but what she was—wise beyond her years, and more precious than a rare gem.

But he tamped it down, determined to be there for her.

"Emma, your work is going to make all the difference for me, for my employees, and for the way this land is used," he told her, his voice gruff from unspoken emotion. "As far as I'm concerned, you're the most important person in Pennsylvania."

She tilted her chin up to look at him and it suddenly felt like the world turned on its axis. In the warm lamplight, he could see the flecks of gold in her brown eyes and the depth of emotion there too.

His heart called out for hers with a desperation he wasn't ready for. How could he feel such affinity for someone whose background was so different from his own?

But at their core they were the same—both fighting to make order out of a chaotic world, both questioning themselves at every turn. He understood her better now, and it only made him like her more.

They had been lost in each other's gaze too long, but he couldn't seem to look away.

"Emma," he breathed.

She blinked up at him slowly and his eyes moved to her full, pink lips.

Every cell in his body screamed for him to kiss her.

With all the strength he had, he managed to resist, turning away from her and putting some space between them.

"I'm glad you like the cottage," he said, placing a hand on the mantle and clearing his throat.

She nodded, but didn't meet his eyes again. She looked almost ashamed, but that couldn't be right. She was probably just relieved he hadn't tried to kiss her.

If he understood her, surely she could read him like a book and she would have seen what he'd just been feeling.

Embarrassed and angry with himself, he strode for the door.

"I should go check on Weston," he told her gruffly. "House is all yours."

He was halfway outside when she called his name.

"Baz?"

"Yes?" he asked, turning back.

"What did Wes want you to ask me?" she asked quietly.

He blinked, trying to remember the person he was fifteen minutes ago, before he almost kissed her.

"Would you like to go out for Chinese food with us tomorrow night?" he asked.

His question hung in the air between them for a moment.

"Really?" she asked.

Her smile was back, along with that hopeful posture.

"Yeah," he said, unable to resist smiling back at her.

"Yes," she said enthusiastically. "Absolutely."

"Very good," he said, his voice a little rough. "See you in the morning, Emma."

"See you in the morning," she said.

Her smile was just as warm and inviting as before, and he felt the heartbroken squeeze in his chest ease a little.

19

EMMA

Emma drove home in a haze, feeling like she must be dreaming.

How else could she explain the magical moment she had just shared with Sebastian Radcliffe?

Just the thought of the sweet little house that he had furnished and gotten ready for her to stay in felt like something out of a fairytale.

She had never really thought she wanted to live on her own, but right now, it felt like an exciting adventure to be able to cook whatever she felt like eating, listen to music late at night if she wanted, maybe even sleep in on the weekend, too.

And the way he talked to her about her work, like he actually *saw* what she was doing and appreciated it.

Well, if she hadn't had a forbidden crush on the man before, she sure did now. There was nothing more attractive than being seen as competent, smart, and valued.

And maybe the feeling went both ways. Her mind went back to the moment when she had been certain he was going to kiss her. His eyes were so intense, that clear blue burning into her soul as he gazed down at her like he was starving for her. Those wild eyes had fallen to her lips, and her cheeks went hot again now just thinking about it, in spite of the frigid air in the truck.

He's your boss, she tried to scold herself. *Pull yourself together.*

But he had wanted to kiss her. She was sure of it.

But he didn't kiss you, she told herself firmly. *So, he didn't really want to after all. Men are so physical, maybe it was just a knee-jerk reaction to standing too close.*

But she was getting to know Baz Radcliffe too well to think that of him. Baz was deliberate, measured. If he had looked down at her mouth hungrily, it meant he wanted to kiss her, at least for a moment.

She made the last turn toward home, and tried to bring herself back to reality as she drove under the canopy of branches.

Maybe there's a spark of mutual attraction, she told herself. *But that doesn't mean I'm a good match for him. He's from another world, that's probably what he was remembering when he decided not to kiss me after all. And that's just fine. In another month or so, I'll be done with the project, and we'll go our separate ways.*

Feeling more grounded, she turned into the Williams Homestead drive. She wasn't looking forward to talking with her parents about moving out temporarily, but thankfully, they were volunteering at the community center in the village tonight, so she could leave a note and put off the real talk until tomorrow.

And while it was awful that the roof was leaking, it meant that most of her belongings were already in plastic bins that she'd carried down to the second-floor guest room.

With any luck, this should be a quick enough move that

she would have time to fix herself some supper when she got back to Whispering Ridge.

She pulled up and parked the truck, then slipped in the front door, taking a moment to greet old Chester, the tabby cat, before she headed up.

The work was quick, and she was just coming down with the last of the bins when she spotted her brother Ansel's truck pulling in beside hers.

"Hey," he yelled to her, giving her a wave as he got out of the truck and walked over to her.

She smiled and gave him a nod, since her hands were too full to wave.

"I was heading home and saw all that stuff in the truck," he said. "What are you doing?"

"I'm moving up to Whispering Ridge until the project is done," she told him, bracing herself for disapproval as she placed the last bin in her truck.

"Yeah?" he asked, looking concerned. "Why is that?"

"I'm trying to get everything done as fast as I can," she said, grateful that he left his questions open-ended. "Putting in some long hours. It'll be easier if I don't have to come back and forth, especially late at night."

A line formed between Ansel's brows, but her soft-spoken brother didn't say anything.

"Radcliffe gave me a little cottage on the property to stay in," she said, feeling her cheeks burn. "I'm not living in his house or anything."

Ansel nodded, and the line disappeared.

"It's just as well anyway," she went on. "Logan's so mad at me that it's better if I just stay out of the way until the project is done and I'm back on the homestead working."

"Logan's full of hot air," Ansel said, shaking his head. "He just misses you. We all do."

"Nah," she said, laughing. "He misses me pulling my weight around here, that's all."

"Well, sure," Ansel said. "But who else would sing 'Girls Just Wanna Have Fun' before the sun is up to make us smile? And who else tells knock-knock jokes at dinner?"

She laughed.

"No one else," Ansel said a little sadly. "I hope he appreciates you over there."

"Trust me, he does," she said, thinking back.

As far as I'm concerned, you're the most important person in Pennsylvania.

"Well, that's good," Ansel said decisively. "And you can stay there if you want, but you'd better be back here for Thanksgiving, or you'll break your mother's heart. Mine too."

"I wouldn't miss it," she told him, impulsively wrapping her arms around her big brother and giving him a massive squeeze.

He hugged her back and all of a sudden, things felt just right again.

When they pulled back, he smiled down at her.

"Show 'em what you're made of, baby sister," he said.

It wasn't until she was in her truck again, heading back to Whispering Ridge that she realized that she was *going home* to a place that wasn't the Williams Homestead for the first time in her life.

It was a tiny bit scary, but mostly a giddy rush.

She rolled down the window and let the November air rip through her hair as she sang her favorite Cyndi Lauper tune at the top of her lungs, not caring what any other drivers might think.

20

BAZ

The next morning, Baz sat on the back porch with a cup of coffee. Weston sat beside him, munching on one of Mrs. Luckett's amazing apple spice muffins.

"Hey," Baz said. "Emma had an idea last night, she wanted to bring her nephew, Lucas, to visit the farm today since he has the day off school. Would you want to show him around?"

"Really?" Weston asked, looking excited.

"He's two years older than you are," Baz said. "But she told me he's really nice, and he's on the quiet side."

"Does he know how to climb trees?" Weston asked enthusiastically.

"I don't know," Baz admitted. "But he grew up on a farm out this way, so... probably?"

"Awesome," Weston said. "I'll bet he knows how to ride a horse, too."

"Definitely," Baz said carefully. "But you need a grown-up to teach you, so you won't be riding today."

"When can I learn?" Weston asked, his voice taking on that whiny tone again.

"Soon," Baz told him. "I have more news from Emma. She does want to go get Chinese food with us tonight."

"*Yes*," Weston said happily.

Baz smiled down at the boy, who was attacking the muffin again with gusto.

He was glad they'd had a heart-to-heart last night. He wanted to see Weston smiling more.

The horseback riding thing was a puzzle. He had to figure out who taught lessons around here that was safety-minded. Surely Emma would know.

He made a mental note to ask her before Weston had a chance to ask about it again. He could picture going on long rides along the ridge with his son, having more heart-to-hearts as Weston grew. But that would require at least a handful of lessons for Weston, and identifying the right mounts for each of them.

As he sat beside his boy, his phone had been buzzing relentlessly in his pocket, but Baz was ignoring it.

No land deal could be worth missing out on these nice moments with Weston, earning his trust so that he could share the boy's confidences. Weston finished his breakfast and leaned against Baz's shoulder, his warm weight felt so good there, like he was right where he was supposed to be.

Single fatherhood hadn't come easily to Baz. He'd tended to delegate everything to experts, and wound up with an army of nannies, tutors, drivers, and cooks filling all the boy's needs.

There was something nice about seeing to Weston himself.

He was just thinking that maybe he ought to take over escorting Weston in and out of his online classes and checking his work when Valentina appeared in the doorway.

"Time for class, Weston," she said sharply. "You're going to be late. Make sure you wash your hands and face, remember the camera has to be on."

"Okay, Valentina," Weston said a little sadly. "See you, Dad."

"I'll walk up with you," Baz offered, moving to get up.

"Oh, no you won't," Valentina said sternly. "You've been ignoring your phone and emails all morning, and you and I have a lot of catching up to do."

"Fine," Baz said, sighing. "Come on. We'll catch up in my office."

Weston scrambled upstairs and Baz headed into his glassy workspace, looking longingly out at the fields, as if he could will a pair of horses to appear to carry him and Weston away from their respective responsibilities.

"Sit," he told Valentina as he lowered himself into his chair. "Is it Larry Bryce? Did he call again."

"About a million times," she said, not sitting. "But first, you and I need to talk about your *consultant*."

He didn't love the way she landed on that last word, as if implying that Emma Williams wasn't a real consultant.

But Valentina was insightful and loyal, so he had to give her the benefit of the doubt and listen if there was something she was concerned about.

"What's going on?" he asked calmly.

"The demands she's making about moving employees around are getting more intense," Valentina said.

"They aren't demands," Baz reminded her. "They're recommendations, and that's what she'd supposed to be doing."

"They're worded strongly," Valentina said.

"Good," Baz told her. "I want to know what she really thinks. That's what I'm paying her for."

"She's inexperienced," Valentina said. "For example, take a look at the guy on line ninety-one. He's one of the few here with a bachelor's degree and he's in a leadership role."

"*Amos Krantz*," Baz read.

"She wants to demote him from foreman," Valentina said. "And she's suggesting that number twenty-seven take his place. Twenty-seven doesn't even show a high school diploma."

"Hey there," Emma's voice came from the doorway. "I can explain, if you want."

"Please," Baz said, gesturing for her to come in.

Valentina stepped to the side, looking mortified and angry.

"Amos is a great guy," Emma said earnestly. "And he's a hard worker, as evidenced by that college degree. But he can't do anything someone else doesn't tell him to do, and he hates making decisions. He's miserable in that job as foreman. But he'd be a real asset reporting to Hal Jenkins, on line twenty-seven. Hal's a natural leader with a big heart who doesn't mind making a tough call in a pinch. The guys love him, he gets things done, and I honestly don't see how a diploma matters when it comes to maintaining a fence line."

Baz buttoned his lips to refrain from hurting Valentina's feelings with an enthusiastic I-told-you-so. She was only trying to protect his best interests, as usual.

"I see," Baz said. "We will take your recommendation under consideration, right Valentina?"

"Of course," Valentina said, nodding curtly.

She was the consummate professional, so only Baz, who had worked with her for years, could see the shame in Valentina's eyes. She turned on her heel and walked out before he could think of how to try to make things right between the two brilliant young women.

The back door closed a moment later, telling him that Valentina had headed out for some fresh air, which was a great idea, in his opinion.

He glanced up at Emma.

"She's way overqualified for this," he said, jutting his chin to the door to indicate Valentina. "Way, way overqualified. I was preparing her to take my place leading the company. When I decided to come out here and pursue a simpler lifestyle, I offered to hand over the reins, but she said she wasn't ready. Then I offered to introduce her to some of the biggest guys in the industry, to get her set up with someone who could get her where she wanted to be. She's a Wharton graduate, worked her way up from nothing. Her family loves her, but they didn't have any money to support her the way other students had, and they had no connections. I met her at a job fair back when I was still doing that kind of thing myself, and she blew me away with her ideas. I've been her mentor ever since."

"No wonder she wants to stay with you," Emma said with understanding in her eyes.

"Oh," he said. "I never thought about it that way. But yes, she wanted to stay with me, even when I came out here. Maybe she thought I would never really go through with it, or maybe it was just how fast it all happened. I had to move so quickly on this once I knew what was going on."

He hadn't meant to say that last part.

"Anyway," he said quickly, hoping she was thinking of Valentina and not his slip-up, "she agreed to come out here, to help with Weston's schooling, and be the liaison between the farms and my offices in the city. It's pretty boring compared to what she used to do. And, like me, she's out of her element, and she's a person who likes to know her business."

Emma was frowning and nodding.

"All of this is just a long way of saying that her concerns aren't personal, Emma," he said. "She's going through a major life and career transition all at the same time. And sometimes it's hard to know up from down out here. But I promise you her intentions are always to make things better."

"I understand," Emma said.

"So, are you ready for a good dinner tonight?" he asked, quirking a brow. "Weston is very excited about giving you a ride in Charlene."

"Yes," she said, smiling. "Absolutely."

But her smile didn't reach her eyes, and she didn't ask who or what Charlene was.

When she turned to go, the thoughtful frown was back on her face.

21

EMMA

Emma spent the day with Baz's words rolling around in her head.

No matter how much she tried to concentrate on work, she was haunted by what he had let slip by accident, and also by what he had told her on purpose.

Valentina's frustration made so much more sense now that Emma knew more. And Baz was blind to what was an obvious truth to Emma.

He saw Valentina as simply loyal.

But Emma knew that if Valentina had spent a lifetime trying to make her way to the top of the business world, without the advantages of connections and money, and as a young woman in a male-dominated profession, then of course she wouldn't want to cut ties with the only mentor who saw her potential and treated her with respect.

Emma could certainly relate. If the whole world had treated her like her brothers did, and then she met someone like Baz, who believed in her, she would have followed him to the ends of the earth.

The whole world wasn't against me, and I still came to work for him.

Emma's heart ached for Valentina, who maybe had made the wrong choice, or at least had made a choice that gave her pain.

Emma was more determined than ever to reach out to the gifted young businesswoman and try to mend things between them. She couldn't offer her a better position, but maybe having a friend would help.

But then there was what Baz had said off the cuff. And he had quickly moved the conversation forward afterward, as if he had realized his error.

Maybe it was just how fast it all happened. I had to move so quickly on this once I knew what was going on...

She could understand a wealthy and powerful man being able to change his lifestyle on a dime, but what did he mean about *what was going on?*

Had he done something wrong?

Or was something going on here in Trinity Falls?

These questions distracted her throughout her day, and by the end of it, she was feeling frustrated that she hadn't accomplished more.

It didn't help that she had brought Lucas over and needed to spend some time helping the two boys find some fun things they both wanted to do, which ended up being a great distraction for her, too.

They'd wound up choosing chess and tree-climbing as their activities, as well as wandering around the farm and *looking* at the horses, but not riding them, since Weston didn't know how yet.

Each time she had checked on them, they seemed to be having a nice time. She found herself wishing all over again that Baz would enroll Weston in the local school. Even though he would be in the elementary school rather than the middle school with Lucas, she was certain that making some new friends would ease his loneliness.

Her phone buzzed at five o'clock on the dot, and she pulled it from her pocket.

> WHISPERING RIDGE:
>
> You'd better not be working ;) Meet me behind the red barn in twenty minutes

Behind the barn?

She laughed and shook her head, figuring he had maybe one more thing to show her on the farm before they headed out. So much for telling her not to be working.

Emma headed back to her dream cottage, stashing her clipboard and pens on her desk, and jogging up the stairs for a quick shower and a change of clothes.

The steamy shower felt amazing, and she came out ready to tackle her off hours with a smile. Mysteries and tricky friendships could be sorted out tomorrow. For now, she just wanted to enjoy the evening with Baz and Weston.

She looked through her clothing, once again stumped by her limited wardrobe of church dresses and jeans.

But thinking about the Chinese restaurant in Trinity Falls village, she decided anything fancier than jeans and a pretty sweater would be silly. Mei Chen's place was lovely, cozy, and decidedly informal.

She dressed quickly and dried her hair, deciding to leave it down. Satisfied, she headed downstairs and pulled on her coat, before slipping out of the cottage.

A strange sound came from outside, almost like a plane was passing overhead. But unlike an airplane, this sound kept going without coming closer or fading away. She wondered if Baz had somehow hired in a farming machine so big and fancy she had never heard one running before. But the closer she got to the old barn, the louder it was, until she heard the chopping sound.

A helicopter.

Emma began jogging, her heart pounding in her chest.

The only reason there would be a helicopter over Trinity Falls was either if something bad enough had happened to make the news, or if some poor person was needing to get to one of the bigger city hospitals in a hurry.

And that second one made her think there had been a farming accident.

But when she ran around the corner of the barn, her eyes couldn't accept what she was seeing.

A sleek, black helicopter sat on the big concrete pad Baz had asked the boys to put in for no reason she could discern, until now.

Baz stood close to the barn, smiling at her, his hair lifting in the movement of those blades.

No one was hurt. There was no bad news.

Her eyes went back to the helicopter. A silver logo shimmered in the setting sun. It was a crest of some kind, with a single word above it:

R*ADCLIFFE*

EMMA FROZE IN PLACE, her mind refusing to compute.

She had known technically that Radcliffe had money. He couldn't have bought all this land and hired all these people without it.

But Emma had known farm owners all her life. Their land might have incredible value on paper, but the owners lived their day to day lives simply, existing off the often-slim annual profits. It was exactly what her own family had done all her life.

This... this *owning* of a helicopter, and using it for no real reason... It was too big, too much.

This kind of wealth frightened her.

"Emma," he said, jogging over. "Everything okay?"

He was the same Baz she had been getting to know, but all of a sudden, the things that had made him different stood out to her again. His clothes were still a little too nice, even if they were simpler than the suit he used to wear, and his teeth were too perfect as he smiled at her. Even his deep voice was modulated and confident, like a movie star.

I don't belong here, a frantic voice in her head cried out.

She was just beginning to shake her head when Wes appeared out of nowhere.

"Emma, isn't it awesome?" the boy yelled in sheer delight as he ran over to join them. *"You get to ride in Charlene. There are special seatbelts, and you get to see the whole world from up even higher than the tree. And then you get to go to my favorite Chinese restaurant, and I can't wait. Are you so excited?"*

He was smiling so hard, and his cheeks were so pink with excitement, that suddenly Emma could breathe again.

"Yes," she told him. "I'm a little nervous, but very excited."

"Awesome," he yelled. "Come on."

She glanced up at Baz, who smiled down at her encouragingly, and then Wes was dragging her toward those rotating blades.

"Keep your head down," Wes yelled, demonstrating.

She let herself be led inside and, just as Wes described, there were very fancy belts to hold her in.

"Ready?" Baz asked her, winking at his son.

She nodded, suddenly feeling terrified, but too curious about this wild new experience to back out now.

Wes handed her a headset, and she put it on, relieved at a slight respite from the sound of the helicopter.

Then they were rising up, up above the farm, high enough to see the farms all around it, and then higher still.

"It's beautiful," she sighed. "I never knew it looked like this—like a quilt."

"You've never been in an airplane?" Baz asked gently, his voice clear in her headset.

She shook her head, then laughed at the surprised look on his face.

"I didn't go away to college, and my whole family is here," she told him. "Where would I go?"

"So many places," he told her.

"You can go to the beach," Wes pointed out.

She smiled at his enthusiasm, wondering how many times he had been up in this thing.

Baz began pointing out landmarks below. Emma was amazed to see the town and the college campus from above. After a time, they were in unfamiliar territory, for Emma, at least.

"So, this is *your* helicopter?" she asked him.

He nodded slowly, almost like he had sensed her freaking out earlier.

"It's really cool," she told him. "I think I like it up here."

That earned her a smile big enough that his eyes crinkled in the corners.

"I'm glad," he told her.

"Did you know that helicopters are really good at bringing water to fires?" Wes asked. "One time, there was a forest fire, and my dad loaned the firefighters Charlene, and she helped."

"No way," Emma said.

"Yes," Wes said. "There were animals in the forest, and it was really important to save them."

"That was very nice of Charlene to help out," Emma said, glancing at Baz so he would know she meant it was nice of him to lend his extremely fancy toy.

"Dad was a volunteer firefighter when he was in school," Wes said proudly.

"Oh yeah?" Emma asked. "A couple of my brothers and cousins volunteer at the firehouse."

A little of the tightness in her chest eased. Baz might have money, but he was still a regular person, too.

The rest of the journey melted past as they talked about the farm, the book Wes and Baz were reading, and his new friend, Lucas.

Suddenly, there was a glittering city below them, and the helicopter was dipping down to meet it.

"It's okay to be scared, Emma," Wes informed her. "But our pilot is the best. He knows exactly how to keep us safe."

That sounded an awful lot like something that had been told comfortingly to Wes a time or two.

"Thank you, Wes," she told him solemnly, trying to hide her white-knuckled hands on the armrests under her coat.

Baz smiled at her comfortingly and she felt her hands relax just a tiny bit.

Soon enough, the helicopter came to a landing. At last, the sound of the motor eased and the blades began to slow. She held perfectly still as Baz came over to pull off her headset and help her with her seatbelt.

He was so close that she could smell the spice of his aftershave. The city seemed to melt away, and she tried hard not to picture him kissing her.

Wes is here with us, and we're just on a visit to the city. We're just friends...

He offered her his hand and helped her down onto a rooftop.

The building they were on top of must have been one of the highest in the neighborhood. Emma looked all around her at the buildings below, trying not to let herself get dizzy or overwhelmed.

After taking a deep breath or two, she felt more grounded.

"Look at all the windows, Emma," Wes said reverently. "Can you believe there's a person behind each of them?"

Sure enough, what looked like millions of windows were filled with warm light. And suddenly, Emma could picture the people behind them. Some business types were working late behind office windows, certainly. But she also pictured families, sitting down to enjoy dinner and each other's company, just like back at home.

"Ready for dinner?" Baz asked.

She nodded and Wes cheered.

"Come on, Emma," Wes said, taking her hand.

They walked over to a simple metal door that opened into a tiny hallway with an elevator.

Wes darted forward to push the button.

Doors slid open to reveal a beautiful interior with mirrored walls and a bronze handrail.

A man in a uniform wearing white gloves, smiled at them.

"It's a pleasure to have you back again, Mr. Radcliffe," the man said. "Which floor?"

"Lobby, please," Baz said pleasantly. "And it's nice to see you too, Phillip."

"Very good, sir," Phillip replied. "And would the young Mr. Radcliffe like to push the button for me?"

Wes practically shivered with delight and reached out to push the L button.

Emma had been in the elevator at the mall on Route 1, but that was only two stories and the glass elevator moved slowly, so you could see where you were. She wasn't prepared for this one, and when the floor simply seemed to go out from under her, feet Emma almost cried out.

"It's a speedy one, Miss," Phillip said kindly. "But you'll get used to it."

She smiled weakly, hoping she didn't look as seasick as she felt.

At last, the elevator stopped and let out a chime. The doors slid open to reveal an opulent lobby.

The ceiling just outside the elevator banks soared to at least three or four stories high, and the floor was gleaming white marble. But it was the people drifting through that open space that made Emma's chin drop.

They were beautifully dressed, like something out of a television show, walking with utter confidence, high heels clicking, not even glancing around at the artwork or the elegance of their surroundings.

She looked down at her jeans and pretty green sweater, and wondered how loud her cowgirl boots would be on those glossy floors.

Baz was wearing a white button down with khakis, and Wes had on a kid's version of the same. Somehow, their attire fit better here, the neutral colors disappearing against the lobby.

For the second time in one evening, that little voice was screaming in Emma's head.

I don't belong here.

"The Chinese food place is right around the corner," Baz told her, placing a hand on her elbow. "I hope you'll like it."

A little tingle went down her spine at his touch, and she went with him, feeling anchored by his big hand at her elbow, and Wes's little one wrapped in hers.

Outside, the cold air whipped at her hair.

"The wind goes between the buildings," Baz explained. "That's why it feels windier in the city. This way."

Beautiful storefronts were lit up with holiday lights already, even though it wasn't Thanksgiving yet. The displays of the various shops showed glamorous outfits, luxurious furniture, sparkling jewelry, and even decadent desserts, all shown off with a holiday spin.

Even the air tasted expensive, but Emma had to admit to herself that she enjoyed feeling like she was on a movie set. She supposed that Philadelphia just before Thanksgiving wasn't exactly New York City at Christmas, but it felt almost like it.

"Almost there," Wes squeaked after about fifteen minutes of walking.

Suddenly, the landscape seemed to change. The items in the pretty windows were now sculptures of dragons or souvenirs, and even the signs were written in another language.

"Welcome to Chinatown," Baz told her, pointing to a magnificent and colorful arch emblazoned with symbols.

"It's beautiful," Emma said.

"It was created with tiles and other materials that came from Philadelphia's sister city, Tianjin, China," Baz told her. "This is one of the most wonderful neighborhoods in the city. I'm excited that you can visit it with us."

"Me too," she told him honestly, though she still wished he had warned her that she needed to dress up.

"There," Wes said excitedly.

He was pointing to a very modest looking door, just off the main street. They headed over, pushing open the door to reveal a small restaurant, dimly lit, and filled with colorful paintings and jade sculptures.

Emma's mouth watered immediately at the incredible smells.

"Mr. Radcliffe," an older lady said, smiling up at him. "Welcome back."

She led them to a nice booth near the window.

Emma looked around and saw that the place was full of neatly but casually dressed families, quietly enjoying a beautiful evening meal. She no longer felt like she was underdressed.

Instantly, she felt at ease, and she couldn't hide her smile, even when Baz began speaking to their hostess in a language Emma couldn't understand.

She turned to Wes and shook her head in awe.

"Wow, your dad speaks..."

"Mandarin," Wes said. "He used to travel a lot for work. He's been all over the world. But now he likes to stay close, so he doesn't miss me too much."

"I definitely understand that," she said.

Suddenly, she felt an ache in her chest for this man, who had so much money, but all he wanted in the world was not to miss a moment with one little boy.

22

BAZ

Baz looked across the table at Emma, who was laughing with Wes while they ate steaming bowls of hot and sour soup.

Something about the moment tugged at his heart, and when he realized what it was, his breath caught in his throat.

Family.

With his parents far away and his wife passing what felt like a lifetime ago, it had been a long time since Baz had this feeling.

He and Wes shared so many happy memories together, but it was really just the two of them. It had been too long since he had watched Wes share a cozy moment with someone else, since he had felt like part of something bigger than just the two of them.

Emma caught his eye for an instant and something warm and sweet passed between them.

She was happy too.

And wow, was she ever brave.

The fact that she had let Wes lead her onto a helicopter

without revealing until they were in the air that she had never flown before absolutely blew Baz away.

She had never traveled, yet she explored the city with such enthusiasm, drinking it all in with those big, dark eyes.

Emma Williams might be young, but she wasn't afraid. And no matter where she was—the country or the city, a barn or a luxury building—she was deliciously, delightfully, unapologetically herself.

And he liked her sweet, funny, energetic self very, very much.

When Mrs. Liu came back, he ordered a big family dinner, so that Emma could try everything.

Mrs. Liu nodded, and smiled at him with such compassion that it gave him another lump in his throat.

Did the owner of his favorite restaurant suspect how lonely he was? Had she sensed the feelings for Emma that he was fighting?

Wes certainly wasn't fighting his feelings. It was clear from the way he was laughing and leaning against her shoulder that the boy felt safe and happy with Emma around.

And maybe that was the most tempting thing of all.

It was one thing to deny himself. But how could he deny the boy anything? How could he not give this a chance if it might mean Wes could have *two* parents around instead of one.

She's too young, the little voice in the back of his head tried to tell him.

But for once, he wasn't so sure it was right.

Emma was responsible and kind, and it was clear that she loved the same simple joys that Baz and Wes did.

He tried to concentrate on the moment, but he kept finding himself watching it from above, wondering if it was really so strange that a vibrant young woman like Emma might fall for a man like him.

"You okay?" Emma asked him suddenly.

"Very okay," he assured her, pulling his head out of the clouds. "Just enjoying seeing the two of you have fun."

She smiled and he swore her cheeks darkened a bit. Then the food came, and everything else was forgotten as they dug into the mountain of savory treats.

It turned out that Emma was a whiz with chopsticks, which made Wes laugh. As usual, she put away an impressive amount of food, trying everything Wes pointed to, and finally sitting back and patting her belly.

"That was incredible," she told Baz. "I want to come back for dinner every night."

"We can do that, if you'd like," he offered, delighted that his money could be put to a use that would please her.

"I was *kidding*," she said, her eyes wide.

He chuckled and she rolled her eyes.

"You were kidding, too," she guessed, only half-correctly. "You should do that more often. I like it."

Wes laughed, tilting his head back like he was drunk on spicy chicken, and Emma laughed right along with him.

Baz was tempted to tell her about one other project he had in the works that he thought she might like. But now wasn't the time to reveal it. Soon, he hoped he would have things nailed down enough to share with her.

"Ice cream?" Wes asked.

"How can you still have room for ice cream?" Baz teased him.

"Second stomach," Wes replied, patting his little belly. "I have two stomachs, Emma. One is just for dessert."

"Ah, that makes sense," Emma said. "I think I must have a second stomach too, because ice cream sounds *amazing*."

Baz slipped up to the counter while they were talking about ice cream flavors, and paid the bill.

"She's lovely," Mrs. Liu told him with a secret smile.

"She works for me," he said, feeling a little embarrassed. "That's all."

"Not for long," Mrs. Liu predicted. "I think she works better as a girlfriend."

Her eyes twinkled with merriment, and he couldn't help smiling back.

A few minutes later, they were back out on the sidewalk, heading toward Logan Square again. An old man was playing the violin on a street corner, the haunting notes drifting through the wintry night air.

Emma stopped, transfixed, and listened with her eyes closed.

Baz watched her, feeling unbalanced by her beauty and the open way she interacted with her world.

When the song was over, she slipped a bill out of her pocket and placed it in the musician's case.

"Thank you, young lady," the man said, his voice a reedy sound that was almost like his violin.

"Thank *you*," she told him. "That was beautiful. I'll never forget it."

She and Wes walked on, but Baz lingered for a moment at the joy in the musician's face. This was the effect Emma had on people, whether she knew it or not. She made them feel *seen*.

How many times had Baz and Wes passed the same violinist, and treated him like part of the scenery? Baz had never once heard his voice before, though he had tossed plenty of coins into that case.

Soon, they reached the ice cream shop, which was

mercifully still open. Wes chose a cone with rocky road, Baz picked chocolate, and Emma asked for peppermint.

They walked slowly along the streets, which were no longer as crowded, enjoying their frozen treats in spite of the chill in the air.

When they reached the lobby of the building again, Emma looked much more self-assured this time, and he felt pride bloom in his chest at the knowledge that the girl he was coming to care for could conquer anything she set her mind to.

23

EMMA

Emma felt like she was floating as they entered the lobby of the big building once again.

As nervous as she had been in the helicopter, and as worried about whether she fit in here in the glamorous city, she had actually had a wonderful time. Seeing that Baz and Wes's favorite spot was similar to Mei's place back in Trinity Falls had made her feel at home right away.

Now, with a full belly, after an evening of laughing with Wes, things felt almost perfect. Except that Baz had gone quiet and thoughtful back at the restaurant.

Had she done something wrong? Or was he just distracted thinking about work or something else?

"Can I go to my room and grab more books?" Wes asked brightly as they entered the elevator.

"Sure," Baz said. "We won't stay too long though. This will be a late night for us now that we're country people."

Wes rolled his eyes, but Emma laughed.

The uniformed man in the elevator, younger than the one they had met on the way down, pushed a button that said *PH*.

"Thank you," Baz said.

"It's an honor, Mr. Radcliffe," the man replied.

Even in this enormous building, it seemed that every elevator operator knew Baz and which floor he lived on.

This time, Emma was prepared for the elevator to rise swiftly. There was a brief sensation like her body was being pressed downward toward her feet. Then the elevator chimed and the doors slid open.

"Good evening, Mr. Radcliffe," the operator said.

Emma heard Baz thank him, and saw Wes darting off out of the corner of her eye.

But she was too amazed by the apartment to really notice. She'd expected a hallway of some kind, but the elevator doors had opened directly into one of the most beautiful living spaces she'd ever seen. The entry alcove she was standing in had the same marble floors as the lobby, covered by what had to be a very expensive, hand-knotted rug. The walls were studded with beautifully framed paintings of the countryside that reminded her of home again.

"The view is pretty cool," Baz said softly. "Come on."

He put a hand on her elbow and led her forward.

The walls of the entry ended, and suddenly they were in a massive, open space. Three walls of floor to ceiling glass laid the city bare before them.

From the roof, the city had looked like a movie set. From the ground it felt warm and exciting.

But here, suspended among the buildings... this view made it seem almost dreamlike.

"I feel like Peter Pan," she murmured.

Baz chuckled, and the deep sound felt like pure warmth washing over her.

"That was a favorite book of Wes's," he told her.

"If he grew up here, I can see why," she said. "Looking out these windows is just like flying over the city, isn't it?"

"Then Trinity Falls must be Neverland," Baz said with a wistful smile.

"Fewer alligators, though," Emma teased. "So, you really were here, with all this, but dreaming of Trinity Falls?"

"Of course," Baz said. "I know to you this all seems new and exciting right now. But I promise that you would feel the emptiness of it, sooner or later."

Once she tore her eyes away from the view, the apartment itself seemed practically empty. Emma wondered how a child was supposed to grow up in it.

Though she was sure they had brought some things to the country house, it certainly wasn't furnished with the kinds of artwork and seating that would make sense in a space like this.

"Does your landlord mind you leaving this place sitting empty?" she asked, suddenly realizing no one was here to care for it.

"Nah," Baz said lightly.

"I don't know about here, but our farmhouse has to be under constant supervision," Emma said. "If something leaks and you don't notice, it can cause real problems, one thing leading to another—it's a real domino effect. You don't want to have a situation with the owner."

"There's a housekeeper who comes in every day," Baz said. "And I own the place, so there's no landlord."

A housekeeper came in every day to clean his *vacant* apartment?

"Oh," she said. "Right. So now that you've moved, are you going to sell the apartment?"

"I own the building," he clarified. "So, I prefer to keep a

flat here for myself. Besides, it's nice to have a place to crash in the city, even if we aren't living here."

She nodded mutely.

Of course, all of that made sense in his world.

But in hers, every facet of it sounded like an excess so over the top it was hard for her to grasp. She felt a prickle of fear under her skin again.

"This isn't how I grew up," he said softly. "So, I know how it all must seem."

Those simple words meant the world to her.

She looked up at him gratefully, and he gazed down, compassion in his eyes, like he understood why this was all hard for her to take in.

"It's how Weston was growing up, though," he said. "And that's why I needed to get out of here. Nothing about this is normal. I wanted better for him than what I had, but this is just too much."

She nodded in agreement.

"Ann would have told me so years ago, if she were still with us," he said, a distant look in his eyes.

"Your wife," Emma murmured.

"I was still building the business when we lost her," he said. "But she used to talk about how when it took off we were going to *live the good life*. I thought she meant this—a life with money and power. But the more time passes, the more I wonder if what she meant was more time together, more happiness. Weston being raised here by a nanny while I worked day and night to accumulate more than any person needs can't have been what she wanted."

"Of course not," Emma told him, her heart aching for his loss.

"Sometimes, I ask her what to do," he said, his eyes on the starry sky over the city.

"Does she answer?" Emma asked him.

"*Emma*," Wes yelled at the top of his lungs as his footsteps echoed on the marble floor. "Look, I have all the Harry Potter books."

"That's amazing," she told him, turning to look.

Sure enough, the boy hugged a massive seven-book boxset in his arms.

"That's what you want to bring?" Baz asked with a gentle smile.

"Yup," Wes said.

"Okay, then let's get out of here," Baz said.

"I don't want to go," Wes whispered, clutching the books to his chest.

Baz's jaw tightened.

"This was really fun, wasn't it, Wes?" Emma asked.

He nodded.

"I had so much fun seeing your old house and going to your favorite Chinese food and ice cream spots," she said. "Maybe you'd like to go to mine in Trinity Falls?"

"Yes," Wes said, jumping up and down a little. "Can we, Dad?"

It took her a second to realize what a big ask that really was. Bringing Baz out in Trinity Falls meant exposing him to all the people who constantly gossiped about him. And worse yet, Wes would be there. Asking them to do that before they were ready was too much.

"I know you're very busy," Emma backpedaled. "I can just take Wes, if you w—"

"Absolutely," Baz said. "How about tomorrow, after work?"

"It's a date," she said.

As soon as the words left her mouth, she felt her cheeks

go warm. Wes ran for the elevator, leaving her standing alone in front of Baz.

"I-I didn't mean—" she began.

But he reached out so gently and stroked her cheek with the pad of his thumb.

"I love it when you blush," he murmured.

Her heart pounded in her ears, and she felt like she was melting from the inside out.

"Come on," Wes yelled. "It's here."

Emma blinked back into reality.

"Ready?" Baz asked, his voice deep and low.

She nodded and they headed for the elevator together. When they got in, she turned around just in time for one last glimpse of the luxurious lifestyle Baz was leaving behind.

The lights in the buildings outside those walls of plate glass glittered and shone. But all Emma saw was a cold, cavernous shell of a home.

She shivered and turned to Baz and Wes, happy that they had found their way to Trinity Falls.

24

EMMA

Emma woke up the next morning feeling energized and ready to work.

Looking at herself in the mirror, she wondered if anyone could guess about the evening she'd had.

I was on a helicopter. Twice.

I visited the city, and even went to Chinatown.

But the thing that made her feel the most transformed was the single moment when Baz had reached out to stroke her cheek.

I love it when you blush...

Those few seconds had changed everything.

The more time she spent with Baz over the last few weeks, the more she liked and respected him, and the more the handsome rancher's kindness fanned the flames of a crush she couldn't seem to shake.

Emma had been ashamed of her secret crush, certain that if Baz suspected, he would be disgusted, or worse, that he would feel sorry for her.

Instead, it seemed that maybe he felt the same.

A little waterfall of excitement slid down her spine,

making her smile and feel like the world might just crack open and show her all its other secrets, too. She practically jogged to the office, ready to put in a hard day's work.

After all, she couldn't exactly date the man if she was working for him. She was more motivated than ever now to help him make a plan to get his investment up and running.

Up until today, she had tried so hard not to want Baz. And that was fine, because saving the big house on the family farm was a big enough thing to wish for. But this morning, with soft sunlight bathing the farm in its glory, she had dared to hope for both.

The day moved quickly, because she stayed busy. She only bumped into Baz once or twice, but his eyes were twinkling when he looked at her, as if they shared a secret.

She was just replacing her files in her desk when her phone buzzed.

> WHISPERING RIDGE:
>
> I don't mean to rush you, but Weston is champing at the bit here ;)

She smiled at the thought, and typed back.

> let's get him some Chinese food to chomp on instead

She jogged up the stairs before he could answer, pulling on her coat.

Baz was waiting at the top of the steps with Wes beside him. They were both dressed in khakis and button-down shirts again, which made her smile.

"Are we going now?" Wes asked her excitedly.

"Are you hungry?" she teased. "Or should we wait until later?"

"Now, now, now," Wes laughed, knowing she was pulling his leg.

"Okay, that sounds good," she told him.

"We'll take my car," Baz told her. "It's parked out front."

"Perfect," she said.

The three of them headed out into the late November afternoon together. The sky was a pale gray with clouds scudding across it, and the air smelled like snow.

"Think it's going to snow?" Baz asked, echoing her thoughts.

"It's early for snow," she said, and then laughed.

"What?" he asked.

"I don't know," she said. "We sound kind of like all the little old men at the feed shop, trying to predict the weather."

"What's wrong with that?" Baz asked, in mock outrage. "I'm going to be one of those little old men one day. I need all the practice I can get."

She laughed, and he used a remote to unlock a bright red, oversized late model pick-up truck.

"Why did you choose fire engine red?" she asked as he opened her door.

"Is it... the wrong color?" he asked, sounding fascinated.

"Black, silver, and white are the most popular around here," she said, shrugging. "Red feels like a choice, that's all."

"My grandpa's truck was red," he said fondly. "At least, it once was. It was more of an orange by the time he drove me around in it. Now I think of him every time I leave the house."

She felt something crack open in her heart. He hadn't chosen the color to be showy, but because he missed his grandfather. It seemed to sum up a lot about Baz.

"That's really nice," she said softly.

He smiled down at her and then closed her door, heading around to get in the driver's side.

"We're up high in this car," Wes told her, as he scrambled in behind his dad. "You can see so much more this way. Isn't that cool?"

"It *is* cool," Emma laughed.

She had never really appreciated that part of driving a truck, since she'd spent most of her life in them. But now she always would.

"Trinity Falls village, here we come," Baz said, starting the engine.

Emma tried to keep hold of the excitement she'd been feeling all day, but now that this was really happening, she could no longer avoid the dread.

It was one thing to go hang out with a new friend, on what might look like a date. But it was altogether another thing when that guy was Sebastian Radcliffe, the most resented man in all of Tarker County.

It was bad enough that Emma had gone to work for him. Now she was going to be seen out socializing with him, too?

Wes is with us, she reminded herself. *Surely, no one in my hometown would sink so low as to do or say anything against the man in front of his child.*

But based on some of the ugly things she'd heard about Baz before she came to work with him, she wasn't so sure.

His actions had truly hurt people, whether he intended that or not. And it would take time to untangle the shortage of workers and equipment in town.

"Penny for your thoughts," Baz offered quietly, glancing over at her.

"Just thinking about how long it's been since I went out

for dinner in town," she lied, not wanting to discuss what she was really worried about in front of Wes.

"And this will be our *first* time," Baz said. "Right, Weston?"

"Yup," Wes said from the back seat.

"Well, Bowl of Joy is the best Chinese food in the area," Emma told them. "It's also the only Chinese food, but I really think Mrs. Chen's food is lovely. And of course, the ice cream shop is one of my favorite spots in town."

"*Ice cream*," Wes cheered.

"I know we'll love it," Baz told her with a reassuring smile.

She nodded to him and kept her lips buttoned for the rest of the drive.

A few minutes later, Mei had seated them in the nicest booth at Bowl of Joy, and gone off to prepare a feast for them.

Baz and Wes seemed happy as could be, and Wes was delighted with the waving cat that was their centerpiece. But Emma was still feeling a little nervous. She had to consciously stop herself from tapping her foot more than once.

The nicest booth at Bowl of Joy happened to be the one in the window, where everyone walking past would see Emma there with Baz and his son. And when Mei had offered it, the guys were so delighted that Emma hadn't been able to find the words to remind Baz that he had spent all his time in Trinity Falls so far hiding from the rest of the town.

Now, she was dividing her attention between Wes's story about his favorite video game, and the window, where sooner or later, someone walking by would notice she was enjoying dinner at Bowl of Joy with someone they didn't recognize. Word of her new job was surely all over town by now. It wouldn't take anyone long to put two and two together and figure out who Baz was.

The bell over the restaurant door jingled, and Emma saw Holly Fields, the waitress from Jolly Beans head for the counter.

A bag of take-out sat beside the register. For a moment, Emma let herself hope that maybe Holly would pay for her food and leave without really looking around.

But as she waited for Mei to come to the counter, Holly turned to scan the restaurant, and her eyes lit up when she saw Emma.

"Hey," she called to her, heading over. "I haven't seen you around the café at all lately. You've been busy?"

"Hi, Holly," Emma said, smiling back at her friend, in spite of feeling a little awkward. "Yes, I've been working hard. This is Baz, and his son, Wes."

She held her breath, wondering if Holly would recognize that Baz was short for Sebastian. Emma hadn't when he introduced himself to her, so it was possible that she could get through this interaction unscathed, if there were absolutely no follow-up questions.

"Nice to meet you all," Holly said politely. "Baz, is that short for Sebastian? You're new to town, aren't you?"

Wes nodded.

"Yes, ma'am," Baz said.

"Well, I hope you're hungry," Holly said with a smile. "I doubt you'll find better Chinese food between here and China."

Wes laughed at that, and Holly laughed, too.

"Would you like to join us?" Baz asked her.

Holly glanced over at him, her blonde hair sliding over her shoulder.

A sudden flicker of hot jealousy flared in Emma's belly, surprising her.

"Oh, that's so sweet of you," Holly said. "But I'm heading over to my sister's place. My niece was craving wonton soup, and I can't ever seem to tell that little girl *no*."

"Welcome to the club," Baz joked, wrapping an arm around Wes. "Kids are irresistible."

Emma knew that Holly cared for her niece a lot these days since her sister wasn't well. She was about the closest thing to a single parent you could find without actually being one.

She and Baz actually had a lot in common.

Emma willed herself to stay calm and positive. Holly was a lovely person and so was Baz. And Emma had no claim over him.

"Holly," Mei called out. "Everything is ready for you."

"Well, see you guys around," Holly said, giving them all a wave.

She dashed back to the counter and paid, then headed outside.

Emma watched after her, wondering...

Luckily, Baz was talking intently with Wes when Holly passed the window.

She gave Emma a look that said, *Oh.My.Goodness.*

And then she pretended to fan herself as she walked away.

Emma couldn't help giggling, which got Wes's attention.

"What?" Wes demanded.

"Oh, nothing," Emma said, looking away from the window. "I was just thinking of a joke my dad told me."

"I want to hear it," Wes said excitedly.

"What did the ocean say to the beach?" Emma asked him.

"I don't know," Wes said, his forehead scrunching up as he tried to think. "I give up. What did it say?"

"Nothing," she told him. "It just *waved*."

He laughed so hard that she started laughing again herself.

"Easy, buddy," Baz said, but he was grinning too.

They chatted and laughed, trading dad jokes until the food arrived at the table. When it came, Emma waited, eager to see what Baz and Wes thought. After all, they were used to their own favorite spot.

"So good," Wes declared, his mouth full of crab rangoon.

"Table manners, buddy," Baz reminded him.

But then he groaned himself over his first sip of soup.

Emma smiled, feeling as proud as if she had cooked it all herself.

The meal went on peacefully, with only a few other customers stopping in, and none of them really in Emma's circle.

When they were finished, they said goodbye to Mei and headed over to the ice cream shop. It was just Emma's luck that they bumped into Amanda Luckett and Valerie Leighton as they were crossing the street.

"Oh, wow, *hiiiii*," Amanda said to Baz, not even acknowledging Emma, who she had known all her life. "Is my mom taking good care of you guys?"

She knelt down without giving him time to answer, and looked Wes in the eyes.

"Are you doing okay, little guy?" she asked in a sugary voice.

Wes blinked at her, as if uncertain how to respond when someone talked to him like he was five.

"We're doing just fine," Baz answered for him. "And your

mother's a wonderful housekeeper. I'm sure I've put on five pounds since we moved out here."

"Well, a good woman knows how to feed a man healthy food at home," Amanda said, straightening, and managing to slide a judgmental look at Emma and the restaurant behind her, before turning back to Baz with a sweet smile.

"Sebastian Radcliffe," Valerie said thoughtfully.

Everyone turned to look at her, but Valerie apparently had nothing more to say on the matter. She fixed Emma with her cool stare and then nodded once, as if she had pieced something together.

Emma's mother liked to say that Valerie Leighton was a good woman, even if she wasn't warm and fuzzy.

The cool-hearted jeweler lived in a little apartment above her shop and dressed like she was walking the runway in Manhattan, not caring in the slightest that everyone around her was bundled up in cozy winter clothing, appropriate for their rural hometown.

Valerie marched to the beat of her own drummer, and apparently kept her own counsel, too. She turned on her heel and marched off toward the café on the corner, leaving Amanda to jog off after her.

"What a pair," Baz said mildly. "Shall we?"

Emma nodded and they headed for the ice cream shop.

It was kind of incredible, really, that they were bumping into so many single women today. She would have sworn this town was nothing but farmers.

Or maybe you've never had a man to be jealous over before.

She begged her mind not to linger on that thought. Baz wasn't her man.

"Emma," Mrs. Bard called out as they entered the ice cream shop. "So good to see you. And who's this with you?"

"I'm Wes. And that's my dad, Baz."

"Oh, thank goodness," Mrs. Bard said. "For a minute I was afraid you were that awful rancher who's been buying up all the land."

There was a horrible moment of silence and then Baz began to laugh.

"What did I say?" Mrs. Bard asked worriedly.

"I *am* that awful rancher," Baz said. "And now I see it's been a mistake to stay out of the village. Maybe I could have made a better reputation for myself. Or at least a more detailed one."

"Good heavens," Mrs. Bard said, shaking her head. "I am truly sorry. This is a good lesson for me in being neighborly."

"Believe me, I've heard worse," Baz said, sticking out his hand. "Sebastian Radcliffe."

"Penny Bard," Mrs. Bard said, taking it and shaking.

Emma smiled to see the sweet, petite mom of Miss Caroline, the children's librarian, making friends with her unpopular boss.

But Baz had a way of making people feel important. She had experienced it herself, and knew that Valentina had as well.

"Well, since you're new in town, you each get a free ice cream cone, and you can choose the flavor," Mrs. Bard was telling them. "You too, Emma, since you brought them."

"That's very neighborly," Baz said with a big smile.

Emma laughed when Wes chose rocky road again, but sure enough Baz picked chocolate, and when she saw there was peppermint, she repeated last night's choice as well.

"Thank you so much for coming in," Mrs. Bard said, as she handed over the last cone. "And don't be strangers."

"Thank you," Baz said.

Mrs. Bard turned to the sink to wash her scoops and the others headed for the door.

But not before Emma caught Baz slipping a twenty into the tip jar out of the corner of her eye.

Since he didn't seem to want fanfare, she pretended not to notice, but it warmed her heart to think of sweet Mrs. Bard seeing it when she turned back to her counter, and knowing that she was truly forgiven for her harsh words.

He's a good man, she found herself thinking. *A genuinely good man.*

As they wandered out and down the street to check out the little amphitheater by the library, she let herself daydream just a little.

What would it be like if they really were dating?

They'd bumped into two of the prettiest girls in town tonight, and he hadn't given them a second glance. But the way he looked at Emma sometimes...

I love it when you blush...

What would it be like to bring him home to meet her family? What if they shared Thanksgiving dinner with Baz and Wes?

"Emma," Baz said softly as Wes ran off to climb up and down the stone benches. "I wanted to talk with you about something, something big. Is now a good time?"

25

BAZ

Baz had put together six figure deals and taken apart seven figure assets, but he had never felt the prickle of nervous excitement he did now.

Because if this particular deal went through, it wouldn't just be a business investment, it would be an investment in the person he was starting to think he wanted to spend the rest of his life with.

All the reasons he had not wanted to pursue her were still there. She was young and sweet, she worked for him, and he had a child who had to come first in his heart.

But lately, those obstacles were falling away like waves crashing on a shore.

His son loved her, and Emma loved him right back. It was clear every time Baz was in their presence that the two shared a bond that transcended their differences.

It was true that she worked for him, but she wouldn't have to forever, if she didn't want to. And if things went the way he hoped, the land would be half hers one day anyway, meaning that if she kept working, it would be *with him,* not for him.

The gap in their ages and life experience had stopped making him cringe the night he saw her handle their city trip like a pro. Baz was determined to enjoy every moment of helping her build all the life experiences she wanted. And he would be right there at her side, keeping her company and maybe racking up some new experiences of his own. Her enthusiasm and courage out of her comfort zone inspired him to try new things himself.

Things were moving awfully quickly. But if there was one thing he had learned from sweet Ann, it was that life could be so, so short.

He glanced down at Emma and felt all the hope and joy for himself and Wes that he had been experiencing lately every time she was around.

"Sure, we can talk," she told him.

Her brown eyes sparkled in the setting sun and the auburn highlights flickered in her hair. He wanted so badly to pull her close, kiss her and make her his own.

For one breathless instant, he wondered if he could just throw caution to the wind and do it. The sound of Wes's laughter faded with the scrape of dry leaves swirling on the sidewalk. And there was only Emma, and the thrum of her pulse at her neck, the parting of her pink lips as she looked up at him.

He knew to his bones that she was waiting for him to kiss her.

But what he was going to tell her would set her heart at ease, so that when he did kiss her, she would have nothing on her mind but him.

"It's about the Williams Homestead," he told her softly, taking her hand.

She blinked at him in confusion.

"I know, this isn't something we talked about," he told

her. "I didn't want to get your hopes up until I had talked with your parents and walked the land. This would be the biggest investment I've made in Trinity Falls, and I had to be sure I understood the responsibility I was carving out for myself."

"Wh-what?" she gasped.

He realized too late that her eyes had gone wide and her face was pale.

"I know you worry about the farm, Emma," he said quickly. "You worry about your brothers having to run it on their own. I want to take that burden from you. And I'm making your parents an offer—"

"I'm not feeling so good," she said woodenly, pulling her hand from his. "I need to go home."

Suddenly, it made sense why she looked so upset. They had just eaten a feast and then ice cream on top of it. Something hadn't agreed with her, and she was feeling sick. That was all.

He almost smiled with relief. But obviously she couldn't be anything but thrilled to have her worries about the homestead off her back.

"Of course," he told her. "Can you make it to the car?"

She nodded with her lips buttoned.

"Weston," he called. "Come on, we need to go home."

"Emma, what's wrong?" Weston asked plaintively as he dashed back to them.

"She's not feeling well," Baz told him. "We're going to get her back to her cottage so she can lie down and rest. It was probably something she ate."

"We ate the same things she ate," Weston pointed out. "Family style."

That was true. And they both felt fine. But food issues could be tricky like that.

"Ready, Emma?" Baz asked her. "Take my arm."

She shook her head, and headed for the car, walking quickly.

His heart broke for her. She had been having so much fun. And now she was embarrassed. He was determined to get back to the ranch quickly, with as smooth a ride as he could give her.

"Emma, are you mad?" Weston whispered to her.

"I could never be mad at you, Wes," she murmured, giving him a sad smile.

"Don't worry, Emma," Baz told her. "We'll be home soon."

She closed her eyes and leaned her forehead against the window for the rest of the drive, her breath clouding on the frigid glass.

When they reached Whispering Ridge, she scrambled out of the truck and down the path, without even waiting for him to open her door or escort her.

Women are sometimes odd about being sick in front of people, he told himself. *That's all.*

But he watched after her, long after she disappeared from sight.

Had he read her wrong?

A terrible idea began to occur to him.

Was it possible she wasn't sick after all?

Was she disgusted because she could tell he wanted to kiss her? Had it upset her when he took her hand, like it was his right?

Maybe he had been seeing the feelings in her that he wanted to see, not the ones she actually had.

Back in the city, there had been so many women throwing themselves at him. They had only done it because they wanted his money, so he had ignored their advances.

But maybe their attention had caused him to be overconfident now.

A woman of character like Emma would have no interest in taking his money, other than by earning payment for her work, as she was now. He knew in his heart that Emma Williams would only be with a man that she truly respected and cared for.

Sure, she'd been eager to come out with them, but Baz was Emma's boss. How was she supposed to say no when he invited her to do things with him and Weston? How was she supposed to say no when he gazed into her eyes and longed for her openly, as he had tonight?

I've put her in an untenable position.

Feeling like a pig, he turned away at last, determined that he would never make Emma suffer his unwanted advances again.

26

EMMA

Emma spent the following days in a sort of pained haze.

She knew she needed to talk with her parents, but the hurt she felt at them selling the home she loved made it impossible for her to have an adult discussion.

And screaming at Annabelle and Alistair Williams was out of the question. So, she kept her head down instead, focusing on her work and avoiding Baz at all costs.

Wes was harder to avoid.

"What are you doing?" he asked her one day when she was out on the border with the neighboring farm, looking at a big shed that probably needed to come down.

"Hey, Wes," she said. "How did you find me?"

"I climbed that tree," he said, smiling with delight and pointing back toward the farmhouse at Whispering Ridge and a big maple about halfway between.

"No way," she said, smiling down at him.

His chest puffed out with pride. The boy had come so far from the day she first met him.

His button down had been replaced by one of Emma's

brother's old firehouse sweatshirts. Emma had brought it for him, and he'd taken to wearing it almost every day, along with a pair of brand-new jeans from his dad that were wearing in nicely now.

His sneakers were in muddy enough condition that it was clear he was starting to really take advantage of all the places to explore on the farm. All he needed now was a crew of friends.

Emma had always had her siblings and cousins to kick around with. Though probably none of them would ever speak to her again if Baz bought the homestead out from under them.

"Are you eating Thanksgiving dinner?" Wes asked, kicking the dirt with a muddy sneaker.

"Yes," she told him. "I'm going to have dinner at my parents' house."

Maybe for the last time...

He nodded.

"What about you?" she asked.

She truly hoped Baz had remembered to make a plan for the two of them. A week ago, she had been hoping to invite them home with her. Now that seemed like Red Riding Hood inviting the Big Bad Wolf in the front door.

"I think my aunt might come to visit us," Wes said, perking up a little. "And Mrs. Luckett's going to cook our dinner."

Good heavens, poor Mrs. Luckett never got a day off.

"That's nice," she told Wes. "It's always good to share Thanksgiving with your family."

"Dad said you're almost done looking at the farms," Wes said quietly. "Then you are going back to your parents' house."

Not if your dad has anything to say about it, she thought to herself angrily.

"He also wants me to make recommendations after I've analyzed everything," she told him. "That will take some time, too. But I hope I'll be all finished by Christmastime."

Wes nodded, looking glum.

"I'll miss you a lot, too," she told him, giving him a wink.

"You're hardly ever here anymore," he said accusingly.

"Well, your dad owns a lot of farmland," she explained. "Not just this one. I've had to travel around a bunch to make sure I've seen everything and everyone."

"But you're not mad at us?" Wes asked.

"Of course I'm not mad at you," she told him.

"That's what my dad said," Wes told her. "But he doesn't sound so sure about it anymore."

Emma resisted the urge to laugh.

Sarcasm has no place in this house, her father used to say, and his rule had kept arguments more or less civil all her life. There was no need to surrender to bitterness or sarcasm now.

"How's school going?" she asked, hoping he'd be willing to let her change the subject.

"It's fine," he said. "I'm bored. I wish I went to school with other kids."

"That makes sense," Emma said, nodding. "I think you know what I'm going to say right now."

Wes rolled his eyes and nodded.

"Have you talked to your dad about it?" she asked, waggling her eyebrows.

"I talked to him about wanting to go home," he told her. "But it didn't work. He just said I'd learn to like it here, just like he did."

Emma nodded, feeling her heart break a little.

"Well," she said after a moment. "Maybe you can let him know you think you'd like it better here if you could go to school in town."

"It won't work," Wes said quietly, kicking the dirt again.

The idea that Baz could continually ignore his son's loneliness made her angry.

"If he doesn't agree, ask him if he liked it here because he spent all his time by himself," she suggested.

Wes's eyes flashed to hers.

"Just ask," she said, doubling down on the tough love. "Politely. I'll bet you and he both might be surprised at how he answers that question."

"Okay," Wes told her. "I'll think about it."

"*Weston*," Valentina's voice came from the direction of the house. She sounded annoyed.

"Oh no," he said miserably. "I guess my break is over."

"Go on," she told him. "I hope the talk with your dad goes okay. You're an awesome kid, and he'd have to be blind not to see it."

Wes glanced up at her, as if he was trying to figure out if she meant it.

He must have liked whatever he saw. His face broke into a radiant smile and then he suddenly wrapped his arms around her waist and hugged her hard.

She hugged him back for all she was worth.

"He's an awesome guy too," Wes whispered to her. "You know that, right?"

"I know, buddy," she told him, swallowing over the lump in her throat. "I know he is."

"*Weston*," Valentina yelled again. This time she was closer.

"See you later," he said, letting go and dashing for the house.

Emma stood frozen for a moment, wondering how she could hold both versions of Baz in her heart at once—the stern but kind man who respected her and melted her heart, and the wicked thief who wanted to steal her family's farm.

"Go on into the house," Valentina said to Wes from much closer than Emma expected her to be. "I need to talk to Emma for a minute."

Emma headed through the trees toward her voice, and met her in a stand of birches.

"Hey," Valentina said. "You okay?"

Emma blinked at her for a moment, so thrown by the casual question she almost couldn't process it.

"I'm fine," she said, nodding. "You?"

"Fine," Valentina said. "Listen, I know it's none of my business, but my advice is that you need to just hold your head high, and don't let him make you ashamed that it happened or feel bad that it's over. He'll crawl back to you sooner or later if it was meant to be."

"Ashamed of what?" Emma asked, mystified.

Valentina looked at her like she was from Mars.

Suddenly Emma thought back to that morning when she had been heading to her car as Valentina came in.

"Oh," Emma said. "Oh, wow. I think I know what you're talking about, but I can assure you nothing is going on with Baz and me."

"You don't have to tell me anything you don't want to," Valentina said. "But just so you know, as an independent contractor, you wouldn't be in any kind of trouble. It's poor judgement, and maybe even taking advantage on his part, but no one is judging you for anything."

Emma shook her head.

"I know you went to the city with them," Valentina said. "It's all Wes talks about."

"We're friends," Emma said. "Nothing more. But you're right to notice something is going on. I guess I should have known that of course you would notice. You're closer with him than anyone."

Valentina smiled grimly at that.

"I'm furious at him," Emma said. "And it has nothing to do with anything romantic. It's business."

"*Really?*" Valentina asked, looking actually interested for the first time.

"He's trying to buy my parents' farm," Emma bit out.

Valentina looked like she was waiting for something more.

"He's trying to buy everyone's farm," Valentina said after a moment, shrugging.

"My family has owned that homestead for generations," Emma said. "It means everything to us."

"Not to your parents, if they're willing to sell," Valentina said. "And if it means everything to them, he won't make them sell. Believe it or not, he does have morals. He won't try to trick them out of it or blackmail them or anything, like a lot of men in his position might. And he'll pay a ridiculous price if they agree."

"It's... it's just *wrong*," Emma said. "That place is important to us, to our town."

"So, it was okay when he bought other people's family farms, but not yours?" Valentina asked.

That stung.

But Valentina made a good point. Emma didn't love that Baz was buying up all the land, but she had agreed to come and work for him and help him with his project. Maybe she had told herself she could help minimize the damage he was doing.

But in reality, she hadn't really gotten mad until her own

family and friends were impacted—both in the feed shop the day she met him, and the evening she found out he was trying to buy the Williams Homestead.

"I guess you're right," she admitted. "But I can't seem to feel better about it just because you're right."

"I didn't ask you to," Valentina said with a genuinely friendly smile. "I just wanted you to maybe consider that it wasn't personal for him. He's just continuing to do what he's been doing. Maybe if he knew it was personal for you, he would change his mind."

"I'm not going to go crawling to him," Emma said, angry all over again. "And besides, he wouldn't do anything special for me. I'm just an independent contractor."

"Whether anything has happened yet or not, I think we both know better than that," Valentina said with a secret smile. "I do know him better than anyone, but a stranger could see the way he looks at you."

Emma felt her cheeks burn and looked down at the ground, feeling more like a silly country girl than ever.

"Just try to keep an open mind," Valentina said. "He's worth it."

"Fine," Emma said. "Hey, it's nice to talk to you about something besides HR. Any chance you'd want to grab lunch sometime?"

"That sounds good," Valentina said, looking genuinely pleased. "But I'd better go find Weston now and make sure he gets into his class on time. Catch you later."

She jogged for the house, and Emma walked after her slowly, looking at the sprawling farmhouse that was Baz's office and home with fresh eyes.

It had once been some family's dream, overflowing with children, glowing lights in the windows in the evenings, lush summers, brilliant falls, snowy winters with snowmen in the front yard, banner years and lean years, and someone carefully scraping and painting the porches and climbing up on a ladder cleaning out the gutters while their loved ones admonished them to be careful, for heaven's sake.

Now that family was gone, and the house stood alone with its memories.

But all of it had still happened.

And Baz and Wes would build new memories here.

Could she ever look at her own beloved family home with that perspective? Could she accept the heartbreak and the happiness at once?

27

EMMA

Emma sat at the Thanksgiving table, drinking in the faces of her family, and all the rich scents of the incredible feast.

Her mother had seated her beside her own place at the foot of the table, next to Logan.

Three weeks ago, putting Emma beside Logan might have been a disaster, but today her rowdy brother seemed to only have eyes for the woman across from him.

As they all went around the table sharing what they were grateful for, Emma felt tears prickle her eyes.

She was grateful for her family and grateful to be back here with them. As much as she loved the cottage Baz had set up for her, this was still her home. She tried not to let herself think about how much longer that might be the case.

When Levi made a proclamation about how some things changed, but that their happiness at spending time as a family sitting around the table together would always be the same, Logan huffed.

"Are you okay?" Caroline whispered to him softly from across the table.

Emma felt her cheeks go hot.

"It's nothing," he said flatly.

"He's mad at me," Emma heard herself say.

"What are you talking about?" Logan said angrily, spinning to face her. "No I'm not."

"Oh, come on," she said. "I know you don't want Mom and Dad to sell the farm, let alone to the man I work for. I might as well be a criminal, in your eyes."

"*Speaking of his eyes*," her mother said sternly, "I'll have you know your caveman of a brother came home with a shiner the other night, defending your honor. So, I suggest you rethink your assumptions, missy."

"Thanks, Mom?" Logan said uncertainly.

After a moment of utter silence, Levi began laughing his booming laugh, and Emma found herself gigging too, as everyone else joined in.

"Couldn't figure out if Mom was defending you or insulting you, eh brother?" Levi asked Logan, wiping a tear of mirth from his eye.

"There's no reason it can't be both," their mother said crisply, rising in her seat.

Then the Williams kids lost it. Even Logan was laughing hard, glancing over at Emma in a way that let her know things were mostly back to normal between them.

"Now Penny," their mom said, turning to Caroline's mother, "would you like light meat or dark?"

The rest of the evening passed in the relaxing way things always did at the farmhouse. They all indulged in the delicious meal and Emma snuck glances around the table.

Josie, her brother Brad's daughter, was chattering nonstop with Lucas, who clearly got a kick out of having her around. On the other side of the table, Levi had slowed his jokes long enough to eat nearly half the turkey all by himself. Her cousin, Tanner caught her looking and winked.

She figured he was doing the same as she was, just enjoying time with the family. There had been enough hardship in his life. It was understandable.

Finally, she looked up to the head of the table, where her dad was gazing at her mom from the whole distance of the feast, love in his eyes so intense it almost hurt to look at them.

Their two guests were deep in conversation with her mother, chatting about community volunteer work. Emma was glad the table was full. There was a lot to be thankful for.

When her dad headed off to brew coffee and her mom invited the kids to help her bring in the pies, Emma got up to stretch her legs.

She found herself heading out to the back porch, listening to the happy clatter of the kids gathering plates and forks in the kitchen, under her mother's instructions.

Emma drank in the cold, still air, and looked out over the farm.

"It's beautiful with the branches bare," her mother said softly from the doorway. "No matter what anyone else says."

"Everything about it is beautiful," Emma said, trying to hold in her emotions.

Her mother walked up beside her, and wrapped an arm around Emma's shoulder.

"Please don't let him take it away," Emma whispered.

"There are some things you should know," her mother said gently. "First of all, the offer Mr. Radcliffe made to us was very generous."

"I don't care if it was generous," Emma said, her jaw tight from trying not to sob. "This is our home."

Her mom nodded and didn't say anything to refute that.

"You know Declan Hawkins, the roofer, stopped by here the other day asking for you?" her mother said after a moment.

Emma hissed in a breath. She had specifically asked Declan not to stop by until she invited him.

"I know why you're working for Mr. Radcliffe," her mother said kindly, rubbing circles between Emma's shoulder blades as if she were thirteen again and her crush had asked her best friend to the Snowball dance. "Emma, it's not your responsibility to put a roof on this house. Your father and I will figure it out."

"By selling it?" Emma asked, then immediately felt bad for being sarcastic. "Sorry. And no, it's fine. I only have a few more weeks' worth of work on his project. I can do it."

"You know he offered to let us keep this house, and your brothers' houses too, and just buy the other buildings and all the farmland and woods," her mother said. "He said he would even hire your brothers on, just like he did with you. They could keep working the land if they wanted."

That actually *was* generous.

For a moment, she allowed herself to consider it.

"It's not the same," Emma said at last, shaking her head.

"You love this place," her mother said, giving her a squeeze. "So do I. We haven't made any decisions yet, but I'll be sure your dad knows where you stand."

"Thanks, Mom," Emma said.

"He respects your opinion, you know," her mother said suddenly. "I know you get treated like the baby around here sometimes. It made me proud as a peacock that you got invited to share your expertise as a professional."

Emma felt seen by her mother so fully and so suddenly it almost took her breath away.

"Yeah?" she asked.

"Yes," her mom said. "Absolutely. Now, are you ready for some pie?"

"Always," Emma laughed.

They headed back inside to where the warmth, laughter, and good smells of Thanksgiving seemed to embrace them.

Emma took her place in front of a steaming mug of coffee and a generous wedge of pumpkin pie, with family all around her.

Please don't let this be the last time we sit around this table surrounded by acres of our own land.

28

EMMA

Emma looked down at the folder in her hand.

Somehow, in spite of the time she had put in—the early mornings and the late nights—when she printed out the results of all that analysis, it felt light as a feather.

In the weeks since Thanksgiving, she had concentrated her work on the final far-flung properties. Mostly because they needed her attention, but if she was honest with herself, she had to admit that it was a relief to stay away from Baz.

He finally seemed to have stopped trying to catch her eye when she stopped in the office briefly to ask Valentina a question.

It hurt more than she expected to know that he wanted her parents' land more than he wanted their friendship to continue. But he had made his choice. And hers had been the inevitable result of his.

There were days when she wondered how she could ever have been attracted to such a cruel and greedy man.

Sure, he was sinfully gorgeous, but she had never thought of herself as a shallow person.

One day, I'll find a man with a kind heart. One who likes me for me, and doesn't care about mining my knowledge or taking my family's land. And it won't matter what he looks like on the outside, because he will be beautiful where it matters.

With any luck, she could begin forgetting all about Sebastian Radcliffe very soon.

After all this time, he still hadn't told her his game plan for the land he had purchased. And that meant that handing over the results of her analysis today was the end of the road.

If he was true to his word, she would have plenty of money to replace her parents' roof and maybe do a few other things around the homestead by this time next week.

And that, she reminded herself sternly, was the only reason she was here in the first place.

Taking a deep breath, she headed into the office wing of the Whispering Ridge farmhouse. Valentina gave her a smile and a wink, and nodded to Baz's door, to indicate she could go on in. The two young women had become friends after all, bonding over coffee and books whenever they could slip away for an hour.

In spite of their different backgrounds, Emma felt right at home with Valentina, now that the highly educated young woman had gained a new respect for Emma's own hard-won knowledge. And she could tell Valentina had let her hair down with her, too. She was a surprisingly funny person when she wasn't in what Emma called her *professional mode,* the mention of which made Valentina cackle. Emma was going to miss her a lot.

"Emma," Baz said, standing as she stepped into his office.

There was a heartbreaking expression of hope on his handsome face that she couldn't begin to understand. He had obliterated all that when he chose her family farm over her.

"I've completed my analysis," she told him woodenly.

"Please, sit down," Baz said. "I want to hear about everything you've learned."

She took a seat on the other side of his desk and opened the folder, trying not to notice the tiniest breath of his aftershave in the air, or the way sitting at one desk felt almost intimate, like they had been before.

"I thought I would go through the property files one by one," she said, looking down at the first one. "I've made notes of what each one needs, in my opinion, and how many workers would be needed to maintain it once it's brought up to snuff. And I've noted which of your current workers I think would thrive in each job for each property."

"Fantastic," he told her, leaning forward with a half-smile, as if he couldn't wait to hear about the fortune in repairs and tear downs he was in for.

And so she began.

At first, she felt a little nervous, going over the facts and figures with Baz listening so intently, only stopping her here and there to ask for more details. But as she went on, she realized that she did have the pertinent information every single time he asked for more, and she began relaxing and enjoying the opportunity to present all she had learned.

After each report, Baz would nod and ask her a few more questions about the property, or say a few words of praise for her effort. The way he was engaging was extremely gratifying for Emma after all her hard work.

In spite of her efforts to keep a wall between them, it felt like Baz was throwing himself against it again and again, until she saw flickers of warm light through the cracks.

When she had finished presenting the final report, Baz sat back in his seat.

"That was incredible work," he told her. "I knew you were a force to be reckoned with the very first time I heard you speak. But this exceeds all my expectations."

"It was a pleasure to work on the analysis," Emma said, pushing the folder across the desk to him, and getting up.

"Where are you going?" he asked, brows lifting.

"Is there anything I didn't analyze for you?" she asked him.

"You were extremely thorough," he told her. "We're ready for the next step now."

Emma could hardly breathe as she lowered herself back into her seat.

Was he about to tell her his plan?

Was she finally going to know what she was doing here, what *he* was doing here, and why the entire farming community had been thrown into chaos?

"I need to know the market value for each of them," he told her, pushing the folder back across the desk.

For a moment, her mind wouldn't accept what he was saying.

Then fury unfurled in her chest.

The big secret plan she had waited to hear about all this time was simply to fix up and resell all these farms, flooding the market and destroying the local economy.

Emma kept her hands in her lap, not reaching for the folder.

"I'm not a real estate agent," she said through a clenched jaw.

"You know the value of this land better than anyone," he told her lightly.

"*Someone* has thrown off market values with their indiscriminate purchases," she hissed.

Wondering if she had gone too far, she glanced up at him.

But there was only humor in his blue eyes.

"Ignore my purchases," he told her, shrugging. "Tell me what each one would be worth if I had never shown up. Assume I'll be making every single repair you recommend in your reports."

Emma wasn't sure she could do this anymore.

Think of your mother's house with those ugly blue tarps over the roof...

Using every bit of self-control she had, she grabbed the folder from his desk and walked out, begging for the patience to get through this without humiliating herself by screaming at him.

"You okay?" Valentina whispered from her desk as Emma emerged.

But she was afraid to speak, so she just gave a weak smile and then headed for the back porch as fast as she could.

It wasn't until she was outside, filling her lungs with the cold, crisp December air that Emma stopped being afraid she would faint or vomit.

I can do this, she coached herself. *There is still a silver lining.*

There wasn't a report on the Williams Homestead in her folder.

At least not yet.

29

EMMA

Emma wanted to scream with frustration.

It was almost Christmas, but her work still wasn't quite finished.

And now, the weatherman had predicted a doozy. Snow was already starting to fall hard, and Sebastian Radcliffe just wouldn't listen.

"We've got flashlights and batteries," Baz said, shaking his head. "There's a shovel by the front door and canned goods in the pantry. Enough is enough."

"How could you send all the farmhands home when there's not enough firewood in the house and there's stuff all over the place outside?" Emma moaned.

"I don't think a snowstorm is the time to worry about tidiness and ambiance," Baz said, sounding a little annoyed himself. "I just wanted to send them home safely."

"When every inch of that land is covered in snow, how are you going to know what you're stepping on if you have to go out there?" she demanded. "Or driving on, if you end up needing to pull your truck up to the house? What about when it starts to melt? How much of that equipment will be damaged?"

"Fine," he bit out. "I'll straighten it up. But we don't need wood. We hardly use the fireplaces."

"Will you use them when the power goes out and your fancy new heating equipment won't work?" she asked. "Or were you just planning to freeze half to death and replace all the pipes when they burst? I know you said money doesn't matter to you like it does the rest of us, so maybe that *is* your plan."

"*Why are you mad at me all the time?*" he demanded suddenly.

She stepped back in surprise.

His own eyes went wide, like he had startled himself as well.

Well, if he wanted honesty, she had a serving of it locked and loaded for him.

"I am *trying* to fix everything for you, just like you asked," she told him. "But I *can't* when I don't know where the goalposts are. I've worked hard for you. Don't you trust me enough to be honest with me about what you're actually trying to do here?"

"I know you're frustrated about that," he admitted calmly. "But you've been frustrated about my lack of a plan since your first day. That hasn't changed. So why are you *mad*?"

His question hung in the air for a moment.

"You're trying to steal my family's home," she heard herself say in a cold, unfamiliar tone.

He only stared at her, looking completely stunned.

"Don't you have enough land?" she asked him furiously. "You obviously have far more than you know what to do with already."

"Is that what you think?" he asked softly. "You think I'm trying to *steal* your parents' land?"

"A lot of people in town think you're just going to resell all this land for a profit when the highway comes in," she told him. "Are they right?"

"Oh Emma," he said, sighing and running a hand through his dark hair. "No. Not at all. It's the opposite."

The opposite? What would that even be?

"If that's true, then why don't you tell me what you're planning?" she asked, trying hard to remain calm.

"Because I'm not planning anything," he said, collapsing onto the chair opposite his desk. "I was only trying to stop something else from happening. After that, I wasn't really sure what to do next."

"What on earth are you talking about?" Emma demanded.

"Coming out here in the summers was the best part of my childhood," Baz said softly. "When things got bad at school in the city, or even later in my life, I would imagine myself here, under the wide sky, with the wind whispering in the pines."

"Whispering Ridge," she said softly, realizing.

"Yeah," he said, smiling fondly. "That's the reason for the name. I always knew I wanted to retire out here one day. Then, as my business saw more success, I knew I'd like to get out here even sooner, while Weston was still at home. It's better for kids here."

Emma smiled and nodded. She couldn't agree more.

"But it wasn't on my radar just yet," he told her. "And I had just pictured us in a nice little house with some land to fool around with."

It might have been what he had pictured, but it certainly wasn't what he'd done.

"Anyway, I was heading out of a board meeting one day and I heard this guy, Larry Bryce, talking about buying up a bunch of land out in the country where they were getting ready to put the highway in," he said. "I knew a highway was going in near Trinity Falls, but I figured what were the chances? I hung around the conference room and listened anyway, and then I heard him say Tarker County."

"Oh," Emma said.

"He said he'd come out this way to scout and that there was a cute little town like something out of a movie," Baz said angrily. "He said he was going to buy up everything nearby and develop it—strip malls, filling stations, outlets, adult entertainment, everything. He said the land was dirt cheap and he was putting together a business plan that would have him retired on an island with a mojito in his hand before it was even fully up and running."

"Trinity Falls," Emma murmured in horror.

"Of course, I recognized Trinity Falls right away by the way he described it," Baz said. "And I couldn't let that happen."

"Baz," Emma whispered, the pieces clicking together for her now.

"I didn't have a plan, Emma," he said sadly. "You were right about that. I've spent my whole career ruthlessly planning every move. But I did this on pure emotion. Including offering to buy your parents' place. You seemed so stressed about having to work that land with your brothers. I thought I was giving you and them choices. I thought I was making your life easier. I didn't mean to make you feel like I was taking anything from you."

That last part was almost too much to take in. Especially when she thought she finally understood what had been happening.

"So, you were just buying all this land to stop him from buying it?" she asked.

"Everything I could," he told her. "But not from people who didn't want to sell. I figured if I offered someone the moon and they didn't take it, they definitely wouldn't take a lowball offer from Bryce. I didn't even need adjoining properties."

"You just had to make sure *he* couldn't get enough adjoining properties," Emma breathed. "*That's* why it looked random from the outside. You *weren't* trying to do anything. You were only playing defense."

"I was trying to save the town from someone else," Baz said miserably. "But I only succeeded in ruining it myself."

"So why do you want to fix everything up?" Emma asked.

"If Bryce comes out here anyway, he could still try to take those properties through eminent domain," Baz told her. "If someone can say that a place is run-down or not being used to its best purpose, they can go to the government, and the government can seize it for other use. Bryce is savvy, he's got connections, and he has the kind of lawyers who could make that happen, or bankrupt anyone fighting it."

"Oh, wow," Emma said. She had heard about this kind of thing, but never imagined it could happen in her own town.

"I figured if I could fix them all up and then resell them at a nice discount below the old market value to people who are willing to work the land, the properties wouldn't be run-down, and they would be in use," Baz went on. "That would make it very hard for anyone to use eminent domain to take them. *And* I'd only sell to folks who were willing to put a deed restriction on the farms that they could never be used for anything but residential and agricultural purposes. That would protect the area for future generations."

Emma just stared at him, speechless.

All this time she had thought he was being greedy, yet he had only been trying to do what she wanted to do when she came to work for him—help the community. He wasn't some outsider who didn't understand. He understood Trinity Falls just fine, and he was working harder than anyone to save it.

"It's probably a stupid plan," he said. "I did it all wrong. And I might lose my shirt on it. But Weston and I will be okay living simply if it comes to that. This is important. It's just taking so long—"

There was a loud thump, and then the power went out.

A small scream came from upstairs.

"Weston," Baz said. "Hang on, let me just get him a flashlight and make sure he's okay."

He disappeared up the stairs, leaving Emma alone with her thoughts.

Guilt fell heavy on her shoulders.

Baz was everything she had hoped he was, everything she could ask a person to be—kind, loyal, selfless, and dedicated to the hometown he loved.

He had even offered to buy her parents' farm, just to help alleviate the stress on her family, and to be sure that they wouldn't sell to Bryce later.

And she had thanked him by yelling at him and treating him like a common thief.

Shame washed over her in waves.

Before she really knew what she was doing, she found herself slipping out the back door and running out into the snow.

The farm was so beautiful that it almost took her breath away, but instead of soaking it in, she ran as fast as her feet would carry her down the path to the little cottage that had finally begun to feel like home.

30

BAZ

Baz looked out the window and saw nothing but the skeletons of trees poking out of the snow, from the back door all the way to the ridge beyond, which looked almost soft under its blanket of white.

It was Christmas Eve, and they were still snowed in.

But that wasn't what had him pacing the floors whenever Weston was busy reading. That was all Emma.

He had come downstairs the other day, after finally spilling his soul to her, and she was just gone. He'd texted her, and she had texted back once, simply telling him she had to get back to the cottage and prepare for the storm, and that he ought to do the same. After that, she'd been silent.

Taking her at her word, he'd set to work clearing up everything out in the yard and carrying in firewood until the snowfall was so thick and fast that it impacted his visibility. He couldn't argue with the results. And with what seemed like and impossible depth of snow, there was no way anyone could know what was under it.

The power was still out, but the living room and den were toasty warm from the fireplace and wood stove. And the heat from the fires was rising enough to keep the upstairs pipes from freezing, so far.

Weston was in heaven sitting by the fire roasting marshmallows and reading his book, stopping every few pages to tell his dad what was going on in the long fantasy saga.

But Baz was filled with a nervous tension that had him checking his phone and the windows constantly.

He missed Emma.

And it was worse than before, because now he realized how blind he had been about her family farm, and how completely he had misread her.

She hadn't been upset that he wanted to kiss her. She had been horrified that he told her he wanted her family's land.

Did that mean she *wanted* the kiss? The idea of that filled him with wild excitement and hope every time he allowed himself to ask the question.

But then what about the other day when he admitted his entire project here was more an emotional reaction than a business decision? He'd thought for a moment that it made her happy, that it helped her understand him better. Seeing her reaction had that same crazy hope rising up in his chest.

But then she'd run.

So maybe he had it wrong again.

"Dad, can I talk to you about something?" Weston asked suddenly from his seat on the rug by the fire. "It's important."

"Sure," Baz said, coming over and lowering himself to the floor beside the boy. "What is it?"

Weston frowned and looked into the fire for a long time.

Baz studied the boy, wondering what was on his mind. He'd asked to talk with such urgency, yet they had been snowed in together for days.

"It's about school," Weston said suddenly. "I want to go to school in Trinity Falls with the other kids."

He snuck a glance up and Baz was blown away by the intensity in those blue eyes that were so much like his own.

"Why?" he asked.

"I know the school you chose for me online is really good," Weston said carefully. "But I think making new friends is important, too."

Baz nodded, looking into the licking flames himself and thinking about sending the boy out into the world, letting it have its way with his precious son.

"I went to school in the city," Weston said softly, as if he could read his father's mind. "And everything was fine."

Baz nodded, knowing the boy was right, but wanting to hold onto the decision for another moment to be sure it felt like the best thing for Weston.

"And I think it would help me like it here better," Weston said softly. "Emma told me to ask you something, if you wouldn't listen."

"Oh yeah?" Baz asked, smiling faintly at the mention of the woman he couldn't stop thinking about. "What was that?"

"She said I should ask you if you liked it out here when you were a kid because you spent so much time alone?" Weston's expression was uncertain.

The question hit Baz so hard that he couldn't respond for a moment.

"I wasn't ever alone out here," he realized out loud, his voice soft with the memory. "My grandfather was with me every minute."

Memories flashed through his head, and he realized for the first time that it wasn't really the farm that made them special. It was Elijah Davies, with the booming laugh and the adventurous soul that led him to bring his adoring grandson on treks through the woods, build bonfires, and fish on the lake for days, all the while telling wild stories about life in the countryside. Time with his grandfather was what Baz had loved about Trinity Falls.

"You loved him," Weston said approvingly.

"Everyone did," Baz said. "He was a wonderful person. He taught me so much. And with your help and Emma's, he just reminded me of something really important."

"What's that?" Weston asked.

"Well, first of all, yes," Baz said. "Of course you can go to school in town. We'll look into it after the holiday break."

"*Yes,*" Weston said.

"It might take time for you to get the hang of things," Baz warned him. "This is pretty different from the school where you used to go."

"Then the sooner I get started, the better," Weston pointed out happily.

Baz smiled at him and wrapped an arm around his shoulder, proud of the boy's courage and his newfound ability to stay positive when things got hard.

The Weston Radcliffe who arrived here a few short months ago would not have found days on end without power to be a fun adventure. Weston had grown a lot.

I have Emma to thank for a lot of that...

"And second of all," Baz went on, "I need to finish with this land project as quickly as possible, because the real reason I wanted to come out here was to spend more time with you. And thinking about my grandpa reminds me that time spent with family is the happiest time in the world."

"What about Emma?" Weston asked suddenly.

Panic fell over Baz like cold water had been dumped on his head. Every single instinct told him to push off this conversation and deny to the boy that Emma meant anything to him beyond a casual friend.

But when he looked down into the boy's eyes, he saw the same hope there that still flickered in his own heart.

"You care about her, don't you?" Baz asked.

"She's the best," Weston said simply.

"She *is* the best," Baz agreed.

"You like her, right?" Weston asked.

"Yes," Baz told him, nodding slowly.

"Like, you *like*-like her?" Weston asked sternly.

"I do," Baz admitted. "But I don't think she feels that way about me. And that's okay. It's good to have a good friend."

"I think she like-likes you," Weston said.

"Why do you think that?" Baz asked, barely managing to restrain himself from grilling the boy. *Did she say so? What did she say about me?*

"Because she looks at you in a different way," Weston said thoughtfully. "She looks at you like she can hear music when you talk to her."

Baz was stunned.

"Do you know what I mean?" Weston asked.

"I do," Baz said after a moment.

They both looked into the fire a while more, lost in thought.

"How would you feel about me having a... girlfriend?" Baz asked at last.

"If it's Emma?" Weston asked.

"If it's Emma," Baz confirmed with a chuckle.

"That would be okay," Weston allowed.

"Good to know," Baz told him. "Good to know."

"She's all by herself at the cottage," Weston said sadly.

They had talked about that a few times already, and it *was* a sad idea. If Baz had only his wits about him a few days ago, maybe he would have found a way to get her back to her family before it started really storming. But the roads had been closed down quickly, and there was no way to get very far right now.

"I know, son," Baz said. "It makes me sad too. I messaged her, but she isn't responding."

"Maybe her battery ran out," Weston said sensibly.

"Oh," Baz said, feeling monumentally stupid. That made perfect sense.

"It's Christmas Eve," Weston said. "And it's not snowing anymore. And we have a shovel..."

Baz was on his feet in a heartbeat.

"*Yes*," Weston squeaked.

"You are to stay right with me every minute," Baz warned him.

Weston was already pulling on snow pants and boots, clearly very excited to go get his friend.

"Hey, Dad," Weston said, looking up from his boots for a moment. "I just thought of something. The blizzard is a memory, right? And we're spending it together."

"Definitely," Baz laughed, feeling his heart melt. "I'm really glad I'm spending it with you."

"But we need to get Emma," Weston said. "She needs to be part of the memory too."

Baz realized he was risking a lot taking the boy out to find Emma.

Please let her be happy to see us, Baz prayed. *Please don't let her break Weston's heart tonight.*

31

EMMA

Emma sat by the fireplace in the little cottage, feeling grateful for dry firewood and a nice collection of paperbacks.

As usual, she had focused all her efforts on practical preparations. When her phone battery almost immediately ran out, she had been wildly grateful to Baz for thinking of stocking her bookshelves when he prepared the place for her.

If only he hadn't shelved quite so much romance.

She had tried reading the cozy mysteries at first, to keep her mind off him and her own stupidity. But even the coziest mystery was a little creepy when she was snowed in all alone.

So, she had started reading the romances after all, and spent the last few days alternately laughing and crying over the stories, taking breaks to check on the pipes and prepare meals of soup and crackers over the fire, as the snow fell, thick and deep outside her windows.

After months of hard work, it was strange to have this peaceful time alone. In some ways, it was healing to have a chance to lick her wounds after humiliating herself over the first man she had ever cared about. But mostly she just missed her family and missed Weston.

And missed Baz.

I wasted so much time thinking the worst of him, even though he showed me he was a good man every single day.

He had been thinking about kissing her in town before he told her he was trying to buy her parents' farm. She was sure of it.

She tried to envision a different way that day could have played out. What if she had *asked* him why he would make her parents an offer on the homestead? What if she had told him she didn't want him to do it?

And what if he had said, *Okay, Emma, I won't. I only want to make you happy.* Would she have thanked him? And would he have wrapped his arms around her and pulled her close for that romantic kiss he had promised her with his eyes?

A shiver went through her.

Shaking her head, she tried to put the fantasy behind her.

She could daydream all she wanted, but none of that was actually what had happened—and she couldn't turn back the clock. She would never be able to answer the *what-ifs*.

She was about to pick up her book again when she heard a thump on the front door.

"What in the world?" she asked out loud as she scrambled to her feet.

"*Emma,*" a familiar voice boomed from the other side of the door, followed by another thump.

"Emma," another one squeaked excitedly. "We came to find you."

"Wes?" she breathed, running for the door.

She pulled it open to find her two favorite guys, pink-cheeked and snowy, outside her door.

"Merry Christmas Eve," Wes yelled, launching himself at her, and wrapping his arms around her waist. "We missed you too much to wait for the snow to melt."

"Merry Christmas Eve to you too, bud," she told him, hugging him back. "I'm *so* glad to see you."

She lifted her eyes to meet Baz's.

He was smiling warmly at her. And maybe it was wishful thinking, but she thought she saw the tiniest hint of longing in those crystal blue eyes.

"Come in," she said, suddenly feeling shy. "I'll bet you guys are ready for some hot chocolate."

"*Yes*," Wes said, letting go of her right away.

"Boots off," Baz called to him.

"Yes, Dad," Wes said, obediently stopping just inside to wrestle his boots off and place them on the mat. "That was a lot of digging, Emma. My dad is super strong."

Baz laughed and the deep, cheerful sound filled the little cottage.

"Not that strong," he told the boy. "And I'm definitely ready to sit by the fire and relax, if Emma's up for company."

"I definitely am," she told him, popping into the kitchen to get the things for hot chocolate.

A few minutes later, she was settled on the rug in front of the fire again, this time with Wes and Baz beside her, each of them sipping a steaming mug of hot chocolate.

They talked about the snowstorm and what the man on the radio had been saying. Emma didn't have a radio in the cottage, so she'd heard nothing and was eager to know more about how the area was faring. It sounded like there had been no serious injuries, but a lot of folks were without power.

Wes told her all about the book he had been reading and asked her what she was reading, and if she had been lonely. She laughed and told him that she was reading all the books his dad had put in the cottage and that they were wonderful company.

The conversation slowed as the hot chocolate disappeared and Wes got sleepy. When it looked like he was about to fall asleep sitting up, Baz took his mug from him.

"Is it okay for Wes to curl up on the sofa?" he asked. "I'd like to stay a bit longer and talk, if it's okay with you."

"If you think I'm sending you back out there, you're out of your mind," Emma told him. "I'll grab a blanket."

She headed for the hall closet and grabbed one of the thick quilts stacked there, trying not to think too hard about what Baz might like to talk about.

Probably just business, she told herself sternly.

When she got back in the room, Baz was helping a half-asleep Wes curl up on the sofa. Emma tucked the blanket around him and he sighed contentedly.

She paused for a moment, wondering how someone so small could be so important to her. When he was snuggled in happily, she and Baz sat on the rug again. Nerves skittered on her skin, but she gazed into the fire, willing herself to stay calm.

"So... your phone ran out of juice?" Baz guessed after a moment.

"It did," Emma told him. "Almost immediately."

"When you turn it back on, keep in mind that you basically disappeared on me in the middle of a conversation," he told her, quirking an eyebrow.

"Will I have a lot of messages from you?" she asked, feeling sort of delighted.

"A lot of messages," he said, nodding and chuckling.

"What did you want to say to me?" she asked.

"At first, I just wanted to know where you went," he told her. "But after that one text where you told me you were safe and getting ready for the storm, I felt better. Then I wanted to know if you had lost all respect for me when you realized I didn't have a plan to turn all this land into some sort of financial windfall."

"Oh," she said, surprised. "It was the opposite, actually."

"Yeah?" he asked.

"Now I know that this place really matters to you," she told him simply. "It feels like your home. And that means we're the same at heart. I mean, I know we're different in almost every other way, but in the way that matters most, we're on the same side."

"The two ways that matter most," he said thoughtfully, turning to watch his son sleeping.

Her heart tugged painfully as she looked at the sweet sleeping boy who changed her perspective on the world every time he opened up to her, and who brought her joy with every smile.

"The two ways," she agreed softly.

"He talked to me about going to school," Baz said, eyes still on Wes.

Oh, good heavens, Emma thought to herself, remembering what she had advised the boy to say.

"What you told him to ask me, about whether I spent my time out here alone, that was a real eye-opener, Emma," Baz said, his voice deep with emotion. "Because I didn't, and I think you know it."

"I do," she agreed, nodding.

"Memories are only as good as the people you share them with," he said simply. "And we want to make our memories with you, from now on, Emma."

She looked to him and saw that he was gazing at her, his blue eyes intent.

"I think you've known that for a while now," he said, his voice a rough rasp. "I care about you, Emma. I look into your eyes, and I see happiness."

Joy pierced her heart, and she couldn't find the words to speak.

"I talked with Wes tonight," Baz went on. "And I can't take any credit, because that boy, for all his hang-ups, led me right down the path to every single thing I'm saying right now. He loves being with you, and so do I. We want you in our lives. I... I want you in my life."

"I want that too," she managed, her eyes tearing up.

"This can't just be for fun," he warned her, his voice suddenly stern. "I'm serious about you, dead serious. And I won't accept anything less."

She couldn't help giggling at him.

"Don't giggle at me," he warned her, his eyes flashing dangerously. "I mean it, Emma."

"This isn't a negotiation, Mr. Radcliffe," she teased. "It's *supposed* to be fun, even if it's serious."

That melted his flinty expression into a warm smile.

"I'll make sure it's fun, too, Emma," he told her, his voice husky.

The firelight glinted in his dark hair and highlighted the sharp, masculine planes of his jaw, which contrasted with the soft expression in his cerulean eyes as he gazed down at her.

"Then, yes," she told him.

"Yes?" he murmured, leaning closer, his eyes sliding down to her mouth.

A shiver of anticipation went down her spine, and she held her breath, feeling almost desperate for him to really kiss her this time.

A moment later he was slanting his mouth down over hers, tasting her lips gently, almost reverently, as he wrapped a big hand around her cheek.

Emma felt the pleasure of his kiss from her lips to the tips of her toes, like she was filling up with warm light.

"*Did she say yes?*" a sleepy little voice whispered.

Emma pulled back fast, feeling horribly embarrassed for letting Baz kiss her while Wes was right there.

But Baz only smiled.

And when she turned, she saw that Wes was still curled up with his eyes closed, too sleepy to open them.

"She did," Baz told him. "And we sealed it with a kiss, so it's real."

"*Good*," Wes whispered fiercely. "*Don't change your mind, Emma.*"

"I won't," she promised. "You guys won't be able to get rid of me. We're going to have so much fun together, and maybe by next Christmas, you'll know how to ride a horse, and we'll go on a Christmas morning ride."

But Wes didn't answer.

"He's asleep," Baz whispered to her. "I honestly can't believe he stayed awake long enough to make sure I talked to you. The minute we got outside he was digging like his life depended on it. We both were. Maybe it did."

She smiled at that idea, trying to picture it.

"I'm so glad you let us in, Emma," he told her ardently, reaching for her hand.

She smiled up at him and placed her hand in his, feeling a shiver of rightness go through her at his gentle touch.

The two of them sat by the fire together for hours, hand in hand, talking and laughing quietly about all their plans for the future.

32

EMMA

Emma woke up Christmas morning snuggled under a quilt, the embers of last night's fire fading in front of her.

She must have fallen asleep sitting up with her back against the couch. But she was leaning on something big and strong and warm.

"Baz," she murmured happily, last night's events suddenly coming together in her mind.

"Good morning, sleepyhead," he whispered.

She felt his lips brush the top of her head and smiled to herself, feeling beloved.

"Did we fall asleep talking?" she asked him in disbelief.

"Well, *you* did," he told her. "Right in the middle of my riveting story about how I learned how *not* to hitch a horse to a cart."

"That doesn't sound like me," she laughed. "That's my favorite kind of story."

"Then maybe I'll tell it to you later," he teased. "But I just got a text from Valentina that they're already clearing the roads."

"Tell me she's not coming in," Emma said, horrified.

"She's a workhorse, that one," Baz said, shaking his head. "But no, she just wanted me to know in case we needed to get into town. And she was checking on you."

"Oh," Emma said. "What did you say?"

"I told her you were just fine, and that we had come to check on you," he said. "Should I tell her anything else?"

"That's okay," Emma said. "I'll tell her."

"Are you going to talk about me when you go out for coffee?" he asked her, winking.

"You're full of yourself, Mr. Radcliffe," Emma teased, elbowing him lightly. "But... yes, probably."

Baz let out a real laugh at that one.

"*Dad?*" Wes murmured from the sofa.

"Merry Christmas, buddy," Baz told him.

"Merry Christmas," he said, popping up. "Is Emma your girlfriend now, or was that part just a dream?"

"Luckily, it's true," Baz declared. "You don't mind labels, do you Emma?"

"I love them," she said, meaning it.

"Me too," Weston decided. "Can we get breakfast?"

"I have an idea," Emma said. "How do you guys feel about meeting my family?"

She kept her eyes sharply on her new boyfriend.

He had said last night that he was serious about her, *dead* serious. But from all her friends had told her about guys, that didn't mean he wanted to spend Christmas with her parents.

Baz's eyes lit up.

"*Awesome,*" Wes said.

"I love the idea, Emma," Baz told her softly. "As long as you're really okay with it."

"I really am," she told him. "But we'd better get dressed quickly. My mom would be so sad if we were too late for a big country breakfast."

"Yes," Wes yelled, hopping off the couch.

AN HOUR LATER, they were almost at the Williams Homestead.

They had waited for Emma to get ready, then hiked back to the big house so the boys could get ready, too.

Of course, they made sure that Wes had time to open his presents, which included a moss green sweater Emma had knitted for him.

"My mom always made us a Christmas sweater," she said, shrugging and feeling suddenly like the present wasn't what a kid like Wes would want, when he opened the brown paper parcel she'd wrapped it in.

"I love it," he told her enthusiastically, pulling it on immediately. "Oh, it's nice and warm."

It was a perfect fit, and the color set off his blue eyes.

"Wow, you'll fit right in at my house," she told him, patting her own red sweater that had been her present from her mom last year.

He grinned at that.

Baz had insisted on taking a minute to put together a little box of candy canes, nuts, and even a scented candle to give to Emma's mom.

Then they had gotten in his truck and headed out.

The plows had come through, but the sheer volume of snow meant the roads were still treacherous.

Baz drove slowly and carefully, and Emma felt safe and sound with the Christmas station on, Wes's voice singing along from the back seat, and the heater pumping out deliciously warm air.

As Baz turned into the homestead and brought the truck slowly down the sycamore flanked drive, Emma began to feel her empty stomach twist on itself.

What was I thinking bringing him here without warning anyone?

Her phone wasn't working, and she knew her mother loved a full house. But it hadn't hit her until now how much this might upset her brothers, or how shocked her parents might be to think of their "baby" dating a man old enough to have a ten-year old son.

"What's wrong?" Baz asked, slowing the truck. "Talk to me."

"I, uh, never brought a boy home before," she admitted.

"And now you're bringing *two* boys home, Emma," Wes piped up. "Will they be impressed?"

Suddenly all her worries seemed silly, and she found herself laughing.

"I think so," she told Wes. "How could they not be?"

"Is this really okay?" Baz asked her. "We can turn right back around."

"No," she told him. "We're not turning around. I'm with you. And I want them to know you."

He smiled and squeezed her hand before putting his back on the wheel and continuing up to the house.

She looked at the snow-covered homestead as he parked the truck. It was so beautiful that it took her breath away every time she saw it like this. All the edges of the trees and the house were softened with snow, and the tarp on the roof was practically invisible.

Too soon, they were jogging up the front steps together, and Emma was knocking on her own front door.

The windows glowed with warm light, and she could hear the music and laughter, even out on the porch. It sounded like every Christmas she could remember, and her spirits rose with hope that on this day of love and gratitude, there would be room in her family's hearts for two more.

Her mom opened the door, with her dad right behind her.

"Emma," her mother said happily, then her eyes moved to take in Baz and Wes.

"Mom and Dad, my phone died, so I couldn't call," Emma began. "But I wanted to... I wanted you to meet, well, to spend time with Baz and his son Wes, they're very important to me."

Her mother's eyes flashed to where Baz's hand held Emma's.

"My dad is her boyfriend," Wes said helpfully.

There was a moment of surprised silence.

Then Emma's mom was bustling outside to take Wes by the hand.

"I'm so happy to hear that lovely news," she told the boy. "I could just tell how much Emma likes you and your dad by how much she talks about you two. Now, you'd better come in out of the cold and help us eat this big breakfast we all made. And the other kids are going to want to see you, too. Do you like pancakes?"

They disappeared into the hustle-bustle of the house, leaving Emma and Baz alone with her dad.

"Nice to meet you under different circumstances," Emma's dad said, extending his hand to Baz.

"You too, sir," Baz said, shaking his hand.

"I won't be selling my land after all," Emma's dad told him.

"Understood," Baz said. "And I'm glad to hear it."

"You're aware that's the baby of our family you're here with?" her dad asked. "And that she's got a passel of doting older brothers?"

Emma was shocked to hear her gentle father say the word *doting* as if it really meant *protective*.

"They'll come to find out that I know how lucky I am and will always treat her accordingly," Baz told him solemnly. "But until that time, I'm prepared to pay my dues."

"Well, no time like the present then," her dad told him with a smile, pulling the door wide open.

And in spite of how impossible things had seemed a few minutes ago, Emma felt at peace now that she had her parents' blessing.

She stepped into the foyer with Baz by her side. Her father closed the front door, and then wrapped an arm around Emma's shoulder and walked them back to the dining room.

The table was full, just the way her mother liked it, with a children's table off to the side, where Wes already sat with Lucas and Josie, the three of them talking excitedly.

Everyone went quiet when Emma walked in with Baz.

Emma's heart dropped to her stomach. She searched the table for Logan, bracing herself for his glare.

But her brother only smiled warmly at her when their eyes met. In fact, he seemed to be happier than she'd seen him in a long time.

Emma felt a weight fall off her shoulders, leaving her light as air.

"Word to the wise, Emma," her father announced. "Your brothers have a truckload of good news for you today. So, you'd better sit down and grab some food before they start sharing it."

Everyone began laughing, and Emma glanced up at Baz. His blue eyes twinkled as he squeezed her hand.

They were home. Together.

And everything was going to be okay.

33

EMMA

A few weeks after Christmas, Emma sat on the sofa of her cottage, texting with her mom while Wes leaned on her shoulder, reading his latest book.

Baz sat at the little table she used as an office, tapping away on his laptop.

It had become their routine to spend more time in Emma's cottage, away from the office and staff. It turned out that the three of them enjoyed the simplicity of sitting by the fireplace even when they weren't snowed in. And while it might be a little cramped for three people, the cottage had an old-fashioned charm that felt like home to Emma.

Today, her mom was excited because Lucy Webb, who worked at the Co-op in town, was having an art show at the library, with a silent auction. Lucy adored Trinity Falls, and she had painted so many beloved local homes and landmarks. One of Lucy's paintings was of the Williams Homestead. It was a hauntingly lovely rendition of the main house, framed by the sycamore lined drive, with the Williams Homestead sign just in the picture.

> MOM♥:
> It's perfect for our foyer, Emma, and we're the winning bid so far! Just a few more seconds now!

>> that's awesome mom

She smiled at the idea of her mother buying something that gave her pleasure. She was a woman who usually made do with last year's dresses, and who could make leftovers last all week in lean times. Emma loved the idea of her having something beautiful to look at every time she came in and out of the house.

Not to mention that it was one more sign that her parents weren't going anywhere.

"*Yes*," Baz said suddenly, leaping up from his laptop.

> MOM♥:
> Oh, no!

>> what happened

"What's going on, Dad?" Wes asked.

"I got them," Baz said delightedly.

> MOM♥:
> Someone else got the painting at the last second!

"Got what?" Wes asked, sitting up straight and lowering his book.

> MOM♥:
> They got ALL of them. Oh, dear. Everyone is so upset.

Emma got a sinking feeling as the pieces slicked into place for her.

"Baz," she said carefully. "You weren't buying paintings in that silent auction, were you?"

"I was," he said proudly. "How did you guess?"

"Did you really buy them *all*?" she demanded.

"Yes," he told her, still having the audacity to look pleased with himself.

"Sebastian Radcliffe, isn't it enough that you bought up half the land in town?" Emma yelled, hopping off the couch. "Did you have to buy all the pictures of it, too? Those paintings mean something to people."

"They're gifts," he said softly.

"What?" she demanded.

He sat back in his chair, looking defeated.

"My grandfather would have pressed palms at the farmer's market, or at church, and talked with people to let them know what he was doing," Baz said quietly. "I guess I've forgotten how to do that. I don't really operate by making friends. I've spent too long making business decisions behind closed doors."

He appeared lost in thought for a moment, but Emma waited, determined to hear him out before drawing conclusions.

She had learned her lesson last time, but it wasn't easy to keep her patience today, when her own mother was heartbroken, and her phone was lighting up with texts.

"I guess people are rightfully afraid of me," he said at last. "I came out here guns blazing, and I haven't exactly made my intentions clear. When I heard about this auction, and went over to the library and saw how beautiful the pieces were... well, I thought maybe if I bought the paintings, and then stopped by and personally gave them to the people whose homes and businesses were in them, it would be a way to introduce myself, and maybe get them to hear me out on what I want to do to get this land back in local hands."

"Oh," Emma said, taking it in.

"I thought I was supporting a local artist. I guess it didn't hit me that they'd all be bidding on their own paintings," he said, lowering his head into his hands.

"That's actually... kind of sweet," Emma told him. "I think you should go through with your plan. I mean now that you have the paintings anyway, why not?"

He lifted his face and met her eyes.

"I promise you that I will not make any more local investments without my consultant's input," he told her. "Well, except maybe *one more,* but it was already in the works."

He pulled something out of his pocket and Wes launched himself off the sofa to join him, looking very excited.

"*Now?*" Wes whispered to his dad.

He had been asking him that question a lot lately, and Baz always said, *Soon.* Neither of them would explain what they were talking about when Emma asked.

"Now," Baz agreed this time.

Wes got so excited it looked like he was vibrating. But he kept his lip buttoned and Emma still had no idea what was going on.

"Emma," Baz said. "We love having you in our lives. Your smile lights up our days, and we're tired of leaving you here alone every night."

He moved to her, kneeling at her feet.

Her heart began to beat like a drum.

"Wes and I talked to your parents," Baz went on. "And

we have their blessing. They mentioned that there is a house on the homestead the three of us might want to fix up and move into. If you say yes."

"You *have* to say yes, Emma," Wes squeaked. "It's your *castle*."

Emma thought of living with the two of them in the great big house with the rabbit hutches and the checkerboard floors, just down the wooded path from her parents, and she felt tears threaten.

"I've made mistakes," Baz told her, his voice husky. "And I'll probably make a lot more. But with your help, I know I can do my best to right my wrongs, and be a better man."

"Oh, Baz," she whispered.

"Will you be part of our family, Emma Williams?" Baz asked her. "Will you marry me?"

He held out a little box that was clearly from *Promises, Promises,* the local jewelry shop. Nestled in the velvet was a sparkling diamond ring.

"Yes," she said, looking down into Baz's intense blue eyes as her heart melted. "Yes, I will marry you."

Suddenly, he was standing, pulling her into his arms, and kissing her like there was no tomorrow.

"Put the ring on, or it doesn't count," Wes yelled frantically.

Emma pulled back, laughing, and allowed Baz to slide the ring onto her finger. Then she grabbed both of her favorite guys and hugged them close.

"I can't wait to be part of your family," she told them, letting the happy tears slide down her cheeks.

THE NEXT DAY, the three of them rode around town, the paintings stowed carefully in the bed of Baz's truck.

Plenty of people were skeptical of Baz when he knocked on their door. But when he handed off his gifts so humbly and asked their permission to explain his plan, most of them invited the three of them in for a cup of coffee or a piece of cake. Ideas were exchanged, potential young folks who might be interested in having their own farm were mentioned, and everyone exclaimed over Emma's ring and congratulated the three of them.

By the end of the day, Sebastian Radcliffe told Emma that he had more new friends in town than he'd ever thought he could earn in a lifetime. There were just three paintings left in the car when they headed out of the village and back toward the countryside.

"Where to first?" Baz asked.

"Well, we've got the Webbs, the Cassidys, and my parents," Emma told him. "Your choice. Mrs. Cassidy will offer you coffee cake. That's her go-to this time of year."

"I guess Webbs first, then," Baz laughed. "That will buy me some time to digest. I'm stuffed already, but there's no way I can turn down Cassidy Farm coffee cake."

They visited the great big modern house the Webbs affectionately called Timber Run, where Leticia and Simon Webb offered them a cup of strong tea, and heard Baz out. Simon's eyes were twinkling with merriment, and when Baz was finished explaining himself, he laughed.

"What is it, sir?" Baz asked.

"Well, a friend of mine called ahead to say you might stop by and that I should hear you out," Simon told him. "I had a good mind to tell him he was barking up the wrong tree, but here we are. I'm glad you came, son."

"Me too," Baz told him.

Then they were off again, to their next to last stop, where

Alice Cassidy did offer them coffee cake, and Baz did make room for it.

Alice cried with joy when he presented her with the painting *Apple Cider Times*, which featured her own family farm. And her husband, Joe Cassidy, slapped Baz on the back and told him to stop by anytime to chew the fat.

The sun was already setting, and Wes had fallen asleep in the backseat as they headed to the Williams Homestead.

"This will be our drive home soon," Baz said thoughtfully.

"Maybe not that soon," Emma warned him. "The house is in shambles. Even the rabbit hutches are half torn apart because we couldn't get supplies to repair the fences."

"I'm so sorry about that," Baz said softly. "I had no idea what I was doing to this town until you came along and made me listen."

"You were saving it," she said simply. "No apologies are necessary. And everyone knows that now. Or at least they will, as soon as the news of your visits hits the feed store and the coffee shop."

"I gave everyone a tough season, and I reserve the right to make it up to them," Baz decided. "But by fall, my farm hands will be free to go back to their old jobs. I'll be done hitting up all the supply houses from here to Philadelphia to fix up all those properties. And you and I will be sipping our coffee on the back porch and watching Wes feed the bunnies at our new house, which I hope will soon be our *only* house."

Emma could *see* it when he described it that way. The man might be over-the-top as far as his drive, but he had a vision like no one she had ever known. She had no doubt that if she agreed that it was what she wanted, every single thing he had just listed would come to pass.

"I really like the sound of that," Emma told him.

"Then I'll make it happen," he promised, his voice husky. "I will do everything in my power to make you happy, Emma. Always."

She leaned on his shoulder, and they spent the rest of the drive in happy silence, pulling into the drive at the Williams Homestead just as the sun dipped below the tree line, turning the sky a beautiful, deep pink, with the swoops and curves of the house silhouetted against it.

A brand-new roof would be installed as soon as the snowy season was over, just like Emma had promised herself would happen when she took a job she didn't want to take to make it happen. But she had never guessed that the people under it for Sunday dinners from now on would include the man who had hired her, and his wonderful son.

"What are you thinking about?" Baz asked her gently as he pulled into his usual spot and parked the car.

"About how I never in my life thought this place could feel more like home," she told him honestly. "But now that you and Wes are here with me, it does."

"Wherever you are is my home now, Emma," Baz told her, cupping her cheek in his big hand. "I'm the luckiest man alive."

As she lost herself in his warm blue gaze, she thought to herself that if he was the luckiest man, then she was *definitely* the luckiest woman.

"All I want to do right now is kiss you," Baz murmured. "But I think your mom is on the front porch waiting for us."

Emma blinked and then glanced at the porch.

Sure enough, Annabelle Williams was standing by the door, peering out into the darkening yard.

"She must have heard about the ring," Emma said,

covering it automatically. "Maybe we should have come here first."

"I have a feeling we did everything in the right order," Baz said mysteriously.

They climbed out of the car, and Baz woke Wes gently.

"Where are we?" Wes asked in a sleepy voice.

"We're at Emma's parents' house," Baz told him.

"Are they my grandparents now?" Wes asked with a smile.

"I guess that will be official after the wedding, son," Baz told him.

"That's nice," Wes said. "Maybe my grandpa will take me fishing like yours did."

Emma could feel Baz's heart squeeze with love for his son.

"Maybe he will," Baz said. "You can ask him, if you want."

"I guarantee he would love that," Emma told Wes. "Ready to head in?"

"But we have a present for Emma's mom," Wes said.

"Right," Baz said. "Here we go."

He carefully lifted the last painting from the bed of the truck. Baz and Wes exchanged a look she didn't understand, but they were both smiling.

"Let's go," Baz said.

"Hey, Mom," Emma called out as they headed for the porch. "I should have called earlier with our big news, but I wanted to tell you in person. I guess the rumor mill beat me to it."

"We're so happy for you, darling," her mother said, catching her up in a big hug. "For all of you."

"Thank you," Baz said, his deep voice filled with happiness. "We have something for you. By now you probably know I realize what an idiot I was about these. Hope you enjoy it."

He held out the painting, wrapped in its protective cardboard and plastic.

"Is this...?" Emma's mom asked.

"Yes, ma'am," Baz told her.

She had tears in her eyes when she took it.

"You're a good boy, Sebastian Radcliffe," she told him fiercely.

"Eventually," he joked lightly. "I'm working on it. At least now I have some help."

But Emma could tell by his expression that he was clearly moved.

"Keep at it, son," her mom replied meaningfully. "You're on the right track."

Then she smiled at him, winked at Wes, and turned to open the door.

An explosion of happy voices sounded from within.

"*Surprise*," Emma's family members all yelled.

Emma laughed with delight as she stepped into the foyer with Baz and Wes, where her dad, brothers, and all their loved ones were waiting to congratulate them on the engagement.

It smelled like they had collectively been cooking up a storm all day and there was happiness in the air along with it.

"We're thrilled for all three of you," her father told her, pulling her in for a hug.

"I think Wes is excited to have grandparents around," Emma whispered in his ear. "On the way over here, he was wondering if you might take him fishing one day."

"Wes," her dad said excitedly, the moment he let her go. "What do you know about fishing?"

Wes looked up at him, his eyes wide with excitement.

"Nothing," he said. "But I want to learn everything."

"That's my boy," Emma's dad crowed. "We'll get you out on the boat this summer, not to worry. Now maybe once this party is underway, the two of us can sneak out to the shed and have a look at the fishing poles."

The two of them walked toward the kitchen, already deep in conversation.

Emma glanced up at Baz and almost got lost in his eyes.

But she knew that this wonderful surprise engagement party was a great chance for Baz to get to know her siblings. So instead of dragging him off to a corner for that kiss he wanted, she graciously shared him with her brothers and their significant others.

Throughout the evening, he would catch her eye, or squeeze her hand, and the look of joy in his eyes told her all she needed to know.

He loved her with all his heart. And the three of them were going to live very happily ever after.

***

Thanks for reading **Rancher's Christmas Cowgirl!**

Want to read Baz and Emma's **SPECIAL BONUS EPILOGUE**? Sign up for my newsletter here (or just enter your email if you're already signed up!):
https://www.clarapines.com/rancherbonus.html

About the next book:

This Christmas in Trinity Falls sure was a doozy—from the

big snowstorm locking everything down, to uncovering the identity of the town's own secret celebrity author, to the (not-so) mysterious rancher buying up all that land. Plus, so much joy and romance for the Cassidy, Webb, and Williams clans that it's hard to believe it was all the same year!

Are you dying to see what NEXT Christmas has in store for our Trinity Falls families? How about starting off with a very special story about what happens when Ian, one of the Cassidy twins, has an old flame show up with a VERY big surprise for him? Want to find out if a secret son and a second chance at love can show this wounded quarterback there's life after football?

Then be sure to check out **Cowboy's Secret Baby**

https://www.clarapines.com/cowboybaby.html